Aces Wild

ACES WILD

Elite Ops #1

EMMY CURTIS

FOREVER
YOURS

New York   Boston

Forever Yours
Hachette Book Group
1290 Avenue of the Americas
New York, NY 10104
forever-romance.com
twitter.com/foreverromance

First published as an ebook and as a print on demand: April 2017

Forever Yours is an imprint of Grand Central Publishing. The Forever Yours name and logo are trademarks of Hachette Book Group, Inc.

The publisher is not responsible for websites (or their content) that are not owned by the publisher.

The Hachette Speakers Bureau provides a wide range of authors for speaking events. To find out more, go to www.hachettespeakersbureau.com or call (866) 376-6591.

ISBN 978-1-4789-4791-2 (ebook edition)
ISBN 978-1-4789-4790-5 (print on demand edition)

For the Command Chief, with love.

Aces Wild

CHAPTER ONE

Royal Air Force pilot Dexter Stone stood outside the hangar and watched the waves of heat undulate above the desert of Las Vegas. He took a deep breath and steadied the jumping in his stomach. It was an alien feeling.

Not only was this the first time he'd flown in a desert environment since he'd crashed his Typhoon aircraft in Iraq, but also this Red Flag training—an exercise that could make or break his reputation—would determine the rest of his career. If he even had one. His career as a pilot, and being a part of the RAF, were everything to him. Everything.

Half of him longed to see a familiar face, and half of him didn't want to see anyone he'd known before. He just had to get through this in one piece and make sure he returned to the UK with all the bragging rights he could get. Whatever the brass said about Red Flag being a collaborative exercise between the air forces of NATO countries and other allied forces, between the pilots and other crew, it was nothing short of a bloody competition. A hard-fought battle of air supremacy, skills, and balls.

And he had all three. At least he used to.

There were two lines of buses waiting to take the military pilots and crew from the hangar area to the auditorium where the Red Flag intro and safety briefings were going to be given. Dex jumped on the last bus, filled with all the other procrastinators.

He took one of the last seats, next to a woman in uniform. American, it looked like, but he didn't want to stare. As people got on the bus, he tried to ignore the nudges and not-so-subtle head nods toward him. *Bollocks*.

A pilot he recognized from Operation Enduring Freedom held out his hand as he walked toward the back of the bus. "Good to see you back, dude," the guy said.

Dex shook his hand and thanked him, then deliberately turned his gaze out the window to avoid anyone else's sad-eyed looks. He'd only crashed a plane, not been held captive. Although that, too, had been a close thing.

As he indulged in his own private pity party, he saw his colleague Clicks emerge from the hangar with a cell phone attached to his head as the bus's doors hissed closed.

Dexter jumped up. "Wait!" he shouted at the driver. He wasn't going to let Clicks miss the meeting and be grounded. He hammered on the window just above his seatmate's head. "Clicks! Clicks!" he called. Against all odds, his colleague looked up and saw him. Dex beckoned.

Click waved, ended his call, and ran to the front of the bus. The driver opened the doors and he jumped on.

"Thanks, mate," he called down the aisle as he took a seat at the front.

Dex gave him a nod and sat back down.

"Did you just call him 'Clits'?" asked the woman next to him.

What? "Did you just say 'clits' to me?" he responded with a barely suppressed smile. "Forward much?" In an instant, all thoughts of his crash, his concern over his career, and his desire to keep his head down flew out the window.

"Excuse me? I was just asking you about his call sign." She sounded indignant, but he had the feeling that she wasn't at all.

"His call sign is 'Click.' Because he doesn't say much when he's flying. Just clicks his mic." He shifted his weight to look at her. "Are you crew?" he asked.

"We're all crew here, aren't we?" she replied, tipping her head to one side.

"Of course we are, just one big team," he agreed, nodding.

She said nothing.

"I'm a pilot," he said. As soon as the words were out of his mouth, he cringed.

Her eyes widened. "Really?"

For a second he thought that he hadn't made a total dick of himself. Maybe he was in with a...

"How *very, very* clever of you," she said, her face giving away her sarcasm.

Nope. He'd made a dick of himself.

He was saved by the guy across the aisle. "Ironman? I thought that was you, man. Good to see you're back. I flew a sortie with you in Iraq. I was on base when I heard about your dirt poisoning. Awesome to see you back on your feet."

Dex ran the guy's face through the very murky filter in his pebble-dashed memory. Then he remembered him. "Grinder, right?" He stuck out his hand. "Thanks."

Grinder shook it and nodded.

"Dirt poisoning?" his seatmate asked.

Fan-bloody-tastic. "It means I crashed." He looked at his lap. He should have made his own way to the mission briefing.

She was silent, but when he looked up, she was staring at him, a frown creasing her forehead. "What was it like?" she asked.

He stared back, trying to figure out if she was taking the piss, or genuinely interested. "It hurt," he said baldly. It had fucking hurt. Both physically and mentally. He'd been able to see the ISIS fighters' faces when he came to. He couldn't get out of the cockpit, and he could see them approaching. He still saw them in his nightmares.

He'd been trying to reach for his sidearm, fighting unconsciousness with all his willpower, wondering if they'd try to take him or if he'd have the guts to use his last bullet to kill himself, when he heard gunfire from behind his position. Pinned in his seat, he couldn't turn around to see if the shooting was aimed at ISIS or at him. It wasn't until a troop had thumped on his aircraft's glass canopy and shouted, "*Ca va? Ca va?*" that he'd realized a French unit had saved him. That was when he'd let go and welcomed oblivion.

"Are you okay?" she asked in a low voice.

His head snapped up. "Sure. Why wouldn't I be?"

Her face softened for a split second. "No reason. Everything's fine." She paused. "Have you been to Red Flag before?"

He took a breath and slid back into his comfort zone. "A couple of times. A while ago, though. Last time I was here, I was flying a Harrier Jump Jet." His favorite aircraft. And a sure-as-shit panty dropper. What's not to love about a plane that can fly at the speed of sound and hover above the bad guys while shooting Maverick missiles?

She nodded thoughtfully. "So, you're older than you look, is what you're saying." She bit her lip, trying not to smile.

He laughed. His Harrier had been retired some ten years before. "Basically, yes. What's your name?" he asked.

"Eleanor," she said, looking out the window and shifting uncomfortably.

She didn't ask for his name, so he decided to just leave it alone. He nodded to himself at his sensible decision. He was different now. More committed to his flying. More careful. Less susceptible to a pretty face. *Yeah, right.* "What do you do?" He could just look at her name and rank on her uniform, like he would have done with a guy, but the Velcro patch that had the information was positioned on the breast pocket. Even he knew better than to snatch a fast look.

She sighed and turned to him. "I'm sure you're quite charming in your own country, but here, you're the enemy. You should get your head in the game and stop flirting with me."

The tightness in his stomach returned. She was right, but

it had been bloody nice not to think about everything that was riding on this week for a few minutes. *Wait a minute.* "We're flirting? You just said we were flirting." He gave her a smug smile and tipped his head to one side. "That's so sweet."

"I said *you* were flirting. Not me." She had a firm conviction about her.

"When was the last time you flirted with someone, then?" he asked.

"A long time ago," she replied shortly.

He leaned in to whisper a reply but got a whiff of a subtle scent that made him think of warm nights and drinks with umbrellas. He inhaled deeply. "Maybe you've forgotten that this is what flirting is like. Maybe I was sent here by some higher power to remind you."

"Really?" She looked surprised. "I suppose you could be right. I could have just spent all my adult years surrounded by men and never once realized what I was missing until you sat next to me on this bus. I mean, it's possible, I suppose."

Dammit. He couldn't tell if she was serious or if she was drawing him up for a spectacular fall. But he liked the way she drew out her vowels; he wondered if she spoke like that when she was turned on too. "Maybe you could meet me in my hangar later...I can show you my Typhoon. You can sit in it if you like."

She gaped in disbelief and pressed her hand to her chest. "Really? Me? In your aircraft? Can I press buttons and everything?"

He was so in, it wasn't even funny. Eleanor was going to be a great distraction, a beautiful, sharp-witted woman who seemed to make him forget all the pressure he was allowing to fuck with his mind. "Of course you can. Just not the ejector seat. That would probably be bad." He grinned.

She looked at him as if she couldn't believe him and then rolled her eyes. *Shit.* He'd been had.

He groaned. Wow. "Well, it was worth a try." He shrugged and gave her an apologetic look.

"Oh my God, could you be any more annoying?" she said with a sigh.

"I definitely could. Let's not forget you started this with all your talk about clits." *Yup, I'm never going to get laid.*

"Now that I know you a little, I'm impressed you know what they are," she said.

He leaned in. "Of course I do." He paused. "I've read all about them."

Gratifyingly, she laughed. "Don't tell me, *Penthouse* reader true stories?"

"Now I'm hurt." He grinned. "But yes."

She laughed again. "What's your call sign?" she asked.

"Big Dick," he lied. "You want me to tell you why?"

"Is it because Tiny Dick was already taken?" she said with fake sincerity.

"Damn. Who told you?"

"Your pants did." She nodded toward his crotch.

"Fair enough." He loved a woman who he could talk shit to like this. He wondered if he would see her again. "Are you going to the mixer tonight?" She might be the only reason he would attend.

The bus's brakes squealed as they pulled up outside the auditorium. The doors opened and everyone began standing up.

"The mixer? No, not my scene. But nice try." She stood up and smiled as if she were encouraging a child.

He nodded and stood back to let her out. *Let's hope that's the only crash and burn I have today.*

The auditorium where their mission safety brief was scheduled to be was decked out in banners and posters for TechGen-One Industries. Major Eleanor Daniels had never seen anything like it. The hallway that ran around the outside of the theater had stands and booths, all manned by people in TechGen-One polo shirts, asking people to sign up for things and giving away tchotchkes. She took a glossy TGO brochure that was shoved at her.

Since when had Red Flag become a commercial endeavor?

Someone brushed past her, nudging her out of the way, and she realized that she had come to a complete halt at the unfamiliar sight. She turned, thinking it might be the British guy from the bus ride. But nope. Shame. She could do worse than engaging in a battle of wits with the big man with his glinting dark eyes.

"Howdya like the idea of 'your mission sponsored by TechGen-One Industries'?" Captain Dickbrain Munster spread his arms as if picturing a banner across the wall. Okay, Dickbrain wasn't his real name, but that was all she had ever called him in her head. He was the juvenile delinquent of the Aggressor Squadron. Not that he was any younger than she was, but he acted like a hormonal teenager pretty much constantly.

She just shook her head, unwilling to engage the idiot-boy.

"Don't be like that. They're awesome. They've already organized a trip for me to spend a week in California at their sim, testing out their next-gen fighter planes. Something tells me they didn't offer you that, huh?" he said, smirking. "Guess you should go to the mixer tonight. See if you can use your female charms to get the opportunities I work for."

Not if you paid me.

She couldn't keep her mouth shut. "Idiot. You'll be too old to be useful by the time the next-gen fighters come on-line," she said. "They're wasting your time and the air force's time. But, hey, it's day one. They were probably going for the low-hanging fruit, right?" She just couldn't help but flap her mouth. Why couldn't she walk away from his shit?

Nevertheless, she had the momentary enjoyment of seeing his smirk falter as the whistle sounded to usher everyone in for the first briefing. As a matter of habit, she patted her flight suit pocket for her notebook and pen—check—as she went to take her seat.

It was a full house in the auditorium. It always was. She spied the insanely hot Englishman she'd been speaking to on the bus sit two rows in front of her. His shoulders were broader than the seat he was sitting in. She bit her lip. He'd made her laugh—inside at least—which was more than anyone else had done since she'd been in Vegas. Red Flag was her test. She was part of the Aggressor Squadron—the team that acted as the enemy during the exercise. It was their job to try to prevent the other units carrying out their missions.

It was a job filled with conflict; she had plenty of friends flying with the allied air forces, most of whom were using Red Flag to shore up their careers. It was her mission to stop them achieving their goals. In order to do her job, and make her career, she had to work to ruin someone else's. It was no wonder Aggressor Squadron didn't have a lot of volunteers.

Now, if she was allowed to fake shoot down Munster, she'd be up for that all day every day. But unfortunately, he'd been assigned to Aggressor Squadron too. She sighed. All that was bad, but what was to come was worse: her father, General Daniels.

He hadn't told her that he'd be there. She couldn't remember him ever being at Red Flag before. But his presence did nothing to forward her agenda of proving she was a worthy squadron commander. Eleanor knew that some people thought she'd gotten her rank because her father was a general. This was supposed to have been her opportunity to show a wide audience that her flying skills had nothing to do with her parentage and everything to do with talent and hard work.

Someone yelled, "Atten—tion," and everyone in the room stood. Her father took the stage. She knew she didn't have to listen to his blather about cooperation and international collaboration, so she found the cute English guy again. At least the back of his head.

She'd heard of Ironman. Everyone had been talking about him for the past year. Everyone knew where they were when they'd gotten news that the legend had been shot down. The hours when they'd all thought he was dead. The excitement when they'd heard he'd been rescued. He certainly hadn't lost his swagger—that was for sure. He even smelled good. Damn.

"As you can see, things have changed around here." The general nodded toward the TechGen-One banners adorning the theater. "This year's Red Flag was going to be canceled due to Pentagon budget cuts, until TechGen-One Industries stepped in, offering to bear all our costs. Quite considerable costs at that, because you guys are not cheap!" He laughed the laugh that only Eleanor could tell was strained, and everyone seemed to love it.

People around her whooped and applauded. Eleanor clapped alongside them, even though the idea of clapping for her father was anathema to her. She hadn't realized that Red Flag had almost been canceled. Thank God she hadn't known. This was the time and place where she was going to prove her worth to the U.S. Air Force, and to her father. She stopped clapping. Actually, the only thing she was interested in proving was that she'd got where she was out of hard work, not because of her father. If it had been canceled, she'd have spent another year twisting in the wind.

So yay. Go TechGen-One Industries. She laughed at herself at her abrupt turnaround. Most military personnel were suspicious of military contractors—that is, until they needed a job. But it seemed as if TechGen-One had the support of the Pentagon right to the top levels. And they may have saved her career. She added her whoop to those of the others. A suited man in the front row stood up. Obviously the head honcho of TechGen-One. He gave an embarrassed wave, then put his hand over his heart as he nodded at the uniformed troops in the hall and sat quickly.

Good for him for not giving in to the temptation to deliver a boring speech when all the people in the room wanted to do was get to their aircraft and compete for dominance in the skies. He also seemed unusually modest for a contractor CEO.

The general handed over the mic to Red Flag commander Colonel Duke Cameron, who with a wave of his hand ordered the visual presentation of the first exercise to be projected onto the glass in front of him. Everyone quieted immediately and leaned forward, eager to get their mission for the morning.

CHAPTER TWO

Dexter leaned forward. He registered a small spike of excitement but repressed it with a firm command. *No. No excitement, no trash-talking, no high jinks—which is what his previous commander had called his exploits before last year's crash...*

These days he had to keep a firm hold on his impulses. The only adrenaline he allowed himself was when he was going Mach 2 toward the horizon. Or talking to a woman on a bus. He had to have confidence in his regulation flying. Not his maverick exploits, not his recklessness, not his gut. His commander had said those things caused his crash.

It was easy to blame pilot error—and it's true he'd been flying so low that a village idiot with a rifle managed to pierce his engine cover—but he'd also been avoiding a surface-to-air missile. He still figured he'd won that confrontation, although it had been removed from the official report because the missile had come from the wrong side of the border. And no one wanted to start a war with the other country because one dude had an itchy trigger finger. So here he was. Having to prove himself again to people who had no idea what really happened to him.

He purposefully blanked his brain and listened to the mission and then to the general when the floor was handed back to him.

"Aggressor Squadron?" the general said.

This was where the U.S. Aggressor Squadron identified themselves to the rest of the allied forces, but no one moved a muscle. No one stood. Dex frowned. Other pilots who'd been to Red Flag before murmured in their seats. Heads swiveled. Still no one stood up.

The general smiled, his bald head shining under the auditorium lights. "No, they haven't forgotten to turn up. They're not hungover—at least I don't think they are."

The audience laughed.

"They are among you. The Aggressor Squadron are among the finest pilots in the United States Air Force, ladies and gentlemen. And for the purposes of Red Flag, they are your enemies. With every mission you undertake, these pilots will be trying their hardest to distract, deter, and keep you from achieving your objective. They may even be spying on you. Trying to get a competitive advantage.

"You won't know who they are. You won't know which aircraft they will be flying. You won't know what their mission is. The one person determined to bring you down…may be sitting right next to you."

It was a speech of showmanship, but still everyone,

including those pilots he remembered from many years ago, couldn't help but turn their head to check out their neighbor. Dex resisted—curiosity didn't change the fact that when he was up there, pilot to pilot, aircraft to aircraft, he didn't care what they looked like. He would achieve all his missions this week or die trying. Because not succeeding would almost certainly mean the end of his career.

The general continued. "This is as close to real-world training as we get. You have an unknown enemy with unknown capabilities. It's your job to work together—the British with the French, the Italians with the South Koreans, the Australians with the Germans. I truly believe that we are invincible when we work as allies." He paused and looked at everyone listening. "Now, go prove me right."

Colonel Duke Cameron stood and led a round of polite applause for the general. Cameron was the mission commander for Red Flag, a job he'd undertaken at least three years ago—Dex remembered flying against him once, then hearing he'd taken over the reins at Nellis Air Force Base. He'd been a bloody good pilot. But damn, how did he transition from combat pilot to desk jockey?

Dex watched him carefully as he spoke again. That could be him in a year if he didn't play his cards right. Cameron didn't seem stressed or disappointed. But who knew? Maybe he had a whole life outside his flying career that held him up when he wasn't upstairs in the sky.

Dex didn't.

* * *

Eleanor enjoyed the anonymity of not being identified as one of the Aggressor Squadron pilots. She exaggeratedly looked around as if she were also searching for her enemy. In her case, though, every pilot in the theater was her enemy. And if she also got to accidentally "shoot down" Munster, she'd take the punishment for that any day of the week. She smiled to herself.

There was nothing in the general's speech that she hadn't heard in one format or another a hundred times before. The theatrics, the repetition. It was as if he always spoke in rhetoric. She frowned. Maybe that was why she'd never felt a connection to him. Maybe her father was all sound bites and clichés? That was something to think about. If she could be bothered. Which she couldn't. Not right then, at least.

Commander Cameron took the podium to outline his expectations for Red Flag. She knew the drill, though. Cooperation, blah blah, fraternity, blah blah, real-world training, blah blah, zero failure, zero accidents—she'd heard it all before.

Commander Cameron stopped talking, and the attending crews applauded and then stood to file out and get in their birds. As the auditorium emptied, her father, the CEO, and two TechGen-One executives chatted in low voices.

She stood to leave, but the general waved her over, barely even looking at her. She walked down the sticky, carpeted steps to the front row.

Still not looking at her, he introduced her to the others.

"Ms. Jacobs, this is my daughter, Major Daniels, one of our top pilots." He said the words with a smile, but why did it always sound as if he was reluctant to say that (a) she was his daughter and (b) that she was an accomplished pilot? Every time he mentioned it, it felt to Eleanor as if he had his arm twisted up around his back almost to the breaking point. "And this is the CEO of TechGen-One, Gerald Danvers."

Eleanor itched to go to her F-16 Viper, but she switched her flight cap from her right hand to her left and shook both their hands. The CEO—Danvers—did seem genuinely nice. He had one hell of a comb-over and a neat pocket square. Old-fashioned. His kind eyes met hers as if he kind of knew what being the daughter of the general was like. She warmed to him.

Ms. Jacobs had a warm handshake and excitement in her eyes. "You're participating? I'm so envious." She grinned at Eleanor, dimples popping in her cheeks.

"Ms. Jacobs here is actually Major Jacobs, retired. She's a Red Flag veteran herself," Mr. Danvers said.

"Please, just call me Casey," she said, her gaze encompassing everyone there, including her boss. "I can't tell you how psyched I am to be here after so many years of being on the other side of the country."

Her father and Danvers continued talking as Eleanor nodded at Casey. "So, was it a good transition between the military and TechGen-One?" She was genuinely interested, as every military troop was, in what came after a twenty-year career. She only had five useful years to go before her retirement. It was a position unique to the military that you could enter into retirement as early as forty. But nearly everyone she knew was already putting feelers out for a job after their retirement.

Casey handed her a card. "TechGen-One couldn't have made it easier. Mr. Danvers is a great man, really. He loves the military and, of course, loves the skills we bring to his business. I've been here for three years and the benefits are out of the world. For example, I'm here because a guy from my old squadron posted on Facebook that he thought the last Red Flag of the year would be canceled due to budget cuts." She shrugged. "I suggested to Mr. Danvers that we sponsor it, get our company in front of a new round of potential employees, and test some of our products here. He just said yes. No ifs, ands, or buts. Just yes. He loves the military, man."

Eleanor was impressed, despite her rule of never being impressed with anything remotely related to her father. "I know I and the vast majority of the pilots and crews here are happy that he does. Thank you." She stuck out her hand again and Casey shook it.

"Call me if you want to chat about your career after the military. Or, you know, if you just want to chat. I remember how difficult it was to be social at Red Flag."

She was right. For female pilots, it was fine to be one of the boys, but when uniforms were off, if was incredibly hard. Female officers always had to walk the fine line of being "fun" but also "untouchable." When adrenaline and booze were involved, it was sometimes better to stay in your lodging than to risk an unfortunate situation.

"I'd like that, thank you," Eleanor said with a smile.

Her father and Danvers were still deep in conversation. She shrugged to herself. She had to go to her mission briefing. She said her goodbyes to the men and strode back up the stairs two by two.

Thank goodness she got away from "alone time" with her father.

The Aggressor Squadron briefings were done in a gray-brick one-story office building at the other end of the airfield, away from prying eyes. Not that it would be the end of the world if people knew that one or the other of them were pilots for the Aggressor Squadron, but the brass liked to try to keep things covert. The element of surprise was key in any kind of aerial combat.

She walked in and took a seat along the wall. As soon as she sat, the mission commander walked in.

Eleanor jumped up and snapped, "Attention," to the other officers in the room who had their backs to the commander. They all jumped up and stood at attention.

The commander—a short but stocky colonel from Hurlburt Field in Florida—continued to the front of the room. "Sit down," he said, and paused until the sound of scraping chairs ceased. "Welcome to Nellis, gentlemen…and lady." He nodded at her.

Eleanor bristled internally but with a neutral expression, took out her notebook and balanced it on her knee. The briefing was fast and easy. The international team was to bomb a warehouse, and a convoy leaving it, in quadrant 46 of the desert range, which was east of the air force base. The Aggressor Squadron was to defend the warehouse and try to disable or bring down the opposing aircraft. Of course, there were no live munitions, as much fun as that would be. All the aggression was virtual; the rest of it was down to who was the best pilot on the day. And that would be her every time.

Eleanor had a plan to win the mission by herself. Because enemies fought dirty—they didn't play by the rules, so she wouldn't either.

CHAPTER THREE

Dexter made his way down to the hangars to check in with the crew, who undoubtedly would already be hard at work.

He walked along the flight line, enjoying the buzz of activity around him. The Australians were playing loud music in their hangar, and it echoed around the ramp area. Dex couldn't hide a smile. This is where he belonged. Funked-up music, bright blue skies, and that familiar feel of anticipation that came with knowing that in a few hours he would be airborne and in control.

People moved in time with the music whether they realized it or not. Mechanics picking up wrenches, weapons specialists walking in time across the ramp, and damn if he didn't see the Australian pilots actually dancing inside the hangar as he passed. He gave a short wave to the pilot he recognized from last year. The guy—call sign Bear—beckoned him over.

"Good to see you, mate. I was worried when you got dirt poisoning last year."

"You were worried? That's so sweet." He reached out and caressed the man's cheek, making Bear dodge out of the way and punch Dex's arm.

"Get off me, mate."

Dex laughed. He held out his hand and Bear shook it.

"Well it's good to see you back. It would be no fun without you," he added.

"Bear, man, I'm not here to have fun. Not anymore. Last year was a wake-up call, you know?" Dex had left his partying days behind. Way behind.

"It's just good to see you, mate. When we heard about your crash, we were sure we would never see you again."

"You and me both." Dex slapped him on the arm. "I'm still going to kick your arse," he said.

"You can try, buddy." Bear grinned and went back to dancing with a couple of female maintenance workers.

Dex tried to put the thought of the crash out of his mind. Even now he was sure he could have prevented it somehow. He'd relived that moment over and over. The incoming missile, ISIS's ammunition warehouse. He'd been trying to lure the SAM to follow him so he could dip behind the warehouse and have the missile take it out as he flew away. Didn't happen like that. He should have flown to a high altitude and shot flares. That was the standard operating procedure.

Dex shook his head and tried to get his thoughts back on Red Flag as he came to the RAF hangar.

Flight Sergeant Matthews nodded at him. "She's looking

good, sir. I've checked her over already," he said, running his hand along the flap of the Eurofighter Typhoon.

Dex had already checked out his plane that morning. He knew it like it was his own child. Every screw, every rivet, every hinge, every marking.

"Are they all in good shape?" he asked, looking at the eight Typhoons in the hangar, parked nose to tail, all gray, except his, which had been painted in the traditional camo of the Second World War, with the RAF target motif on the underside of the wings. It had been painted to commemorate the Battle of Britain, and he felt pride every time he got inside it, as well as a strong connection to those who had fought before him.

Matthews nodded. "They're all ready to give the Aggressors a good spanking, sir."

Dex laughed. "From your lips." Truth was, it wasn't that easy beating the U.S. Aggressor Squadron in their own backyard. They'd spent years practicing over these mountains and valleys. But that was the point. When you were actually flying in combat, you were usually fighting against pilots who knew their terrain like the backs of their hands. This was good practice.

"Just to let you know, I had to stop people getting into the hangar yesterday evening," Matthews said, wiping down a tool and replacing it in the huge metal cabinet they'd brought over with the planes.

Dex took a second. Exploding with fury was last year. This year he was measured, sensible, in charge. "Who was it?"

"TechGen-One Industries. They said they had authorization to be there, but no one had told me, so I asked them to come back during the day. They didn't seem bothered by it. I looked them up, though. Military contractors to the stars," Matthews said, raising his eyebrows. "Everyone uses their products, but they're careful about who they deal with. They only sell to allied countries."

"A military contractor with ethics. That's always nice to hear. Apparently, they're running the exercise this year, so expect to see more of them around," Dex said, wondering if they should make his short list of companies to work for after he retired. Nearly everyone in the military looked ahead to the day they'd have to retire from the forces and find their way in the big bad world. The golden egg was finding somewhere to work that didn't compromise your values.

"I'm sure we'll receive word if they're supposed to be here. I'll go check in and see what's what. Meantime, keep your guard up. Only our team in here."

"Copy that, sir," Matthews said. As soon as he said the words, the pedestrian door to the hangar banged opened.

"Matthews," someone shouted from the doorway. "He's here!"

Both Matthews and Dex poked their heads out from behind the aircraft. The young airman at the door cleared his throat. "I'm sorry, sir, I thought Matthews was alone."

Dex nodded. "Who's here?" he asked Matthews. At his hesitation, Dex said, "Wait. Do I even want to know?"

As if making up his mind on the spot, Matthews grinned. "Hell, yes, you do. The Animal is about to land."

The Animal was a Red Flag legend. "What? Isn't he too

old for this now? Anyway, the South Koreans got here yes-terday. They landed just before I did."

"Yes, sir, they did. But not the Animal. I don't know why."

Probably to make this entrance. The Animal was the star pilot of the South Korean Air Force. Educated in the United States, he was in many respects more American than Korean; he was also the life and soul of any party.

The South Koreans had to fly more than ten hours in their fighter jets from Korea to Las Vegas, not being able to move, not being able to piss except into a bottle, and being refueled en route. When the teams come from flights that long, they usually need to be pulled out of the cockpit, legs and arms stiff from maintaining the same position for hours on end. A lot of times there were also tears of relief when they landed.

But not the Animal. He was in his late thirties and still the total rock star. Dex swore he had the mental age of an eighteen-year-old and annoyingly had the physique of one too. Not only was he the true party animal of Red Flag, but he was probably the best pilot there too.

"Let's go," Dex said.

Matthews wiped his hand on a rag, which he then stuck in his pocket and headed to the door of the hangar. Dex fol-lowed him. He'd have been lying if he didn't admit that he was psyched the Animal was here. He knew this was proba-bly going to be his last Red Flag, and he was happy to see the Animal one more time.

The flight line was packed with people. Dex laughed when he saw the sight. The whole South Korean crew was out waving huge national flags on long poles, the Australians cranked up the music even more, and all the other pilots and crew streamed out of their hangars. All the newbies were being briefed by the Red Flag veterans about the legend. Dex shook his head; nothing they could say would prepare them for the reality.

The Animal's aircraft taxied to the ramp, and as soon as the chock blocks were in place, the plane's canopy pulled back.

The Australians' music changed from dance music to AC/DC's "Back in Black." Dex shook his head. There was nothing in the world that felt more like being on *Top Gun* than watching the Animal get out of his plane. Flags waved, people cheered, and the vast majority of airmen watching raised their arms in the air to cheer him.

Then there was silence. Where was he? Murmurs started. What was wrong? Where was he? The music went quiet.

A few people pushed forward to the aircraft as soon as the engines were shut off, but as they approached the Animal suddenly thrust his arms into the air.

The crowd went nuts. He couldn't believe he was standing here with his flight mechanic watching a pilot get out of the plane like it was the first time they'd ever seen it.

The South Korean put his hands on top of the fuselage and pulled himself out like a gymnast. Arms and head first, followed by his torso and his legs, until he was standing up straight on his hands. You couldn't have made that shit up.

It was a piece of theater, giving the punters what they want to see. With anyone else it would be all exhibition and no substance, or as his mother said, all flash and no trousers.

But with the Animal, this was his whole life. The best pilot, the most fun to be around, the best displays. He was a good friend too.

The Animal climbed down with no stiffness, no tears, as if he had gone around the airfield pattern only once before landing. Dex envied him his stamina and his suppleness. He was pretty sure everyone did.

After greeting a bunch of the other pilots, he saw Dex. "Ironman. What are you doing here? I heard you crashed and burned last year. Weren't you dead or something?" He slapped a shoulder in greeting and then continued undoing a couple of buttons on his flight suit. "You okay?"

"Everything is good, man," Dex said. "Looking forward to testing you this year." He grinned.

"Oh, man, I'll ace every test you give me," the Animal said. "But I'm here for you. If you need to talk, I mean. I imagine it's going to be weird getting up there again after last year."

"That is very nice of you, and you should feel free to come talk to me when I beat your arse."

The Animal laughed, then winced.

Dex laughed. "A little stiffer than you want your audience to see?"

"I'm not getting any younger," he replied, putting his aviators on.

"Your secret is safe with me."

"Come find me later. I'm initiating you into the club."

That didn't necessarily sound good. Any club the Animal was involved in would be raucous, messy, and quite possibly illegal. It was Dex's turn to wince. "Really? It's not going to get me arrested, is it?"

"Where's the fun if that's not a possibility?" he asked with a grin. "Seriously, man, be there tonight. No wait, tonight is the mixer. Tomorrow night. The officers' club. Be there."

Bollocks.

CHAPTER FOUR

Sometimes when Dex was flying, it felt like it was just him and the edge of space. And sometimes, he just marveled at the people who created the vision of an aircraft out of their minds and the scientists who would put it all together to enable him to fly at twice the speed of sound. He loved those moments when he felt the pull of the great blue yonder, when his aircraft defied gravity, desperate to get off the mundane earth.

Above the clouds, above the cities, above the noise. That was where he belonged. Away from everything.

"Blue Sniper One, cleared for takeoff," the controller said in his ears. He moved the throttle forward in a well-practiced gesture, smoothly and elegantly. He felt the aircraft fight to get off the ground before it had reached its correct speed.

The forces of the thrust anchored him to his seat, allowing any tension to disappear. He took a deep breath and lifted the aircraft from the tarmac as if it were a paper plane. Effortlessly, it took to the sky. He pulled an almost vertical departure from the airfield and as he did, he smiled to himself and swiveled his head to see the airport, already fading into the distance under him.

His first mission was to bomb a convoy of trucks. He didn't know where they were; the coordinates would be given to him while he was flying. There were two other Brits with him and one German pilot, all with the same assignment—either to bomb the convoy or facilitate the bombing of the convoy. That meant acting as a distraction, sacrificing yourself in the fight, or drawing fire away from the pilot with the greatest chance of completing the mission.

They had no idea what the convoy would look like, whether they'd be shot at, or what the situation would be—just like real-world conflict.

"Blue Sniper One, I have you in my sights." His colleague's voice came through his headset.

"This is Blue Three, also in sight."

"Ditto Blue Four," his remaining colleague said.

"Copy that," he replied. "I think we've got ourselves a convoy." Dex smiled. This was his happy place.

"Roger that, sir." Blue Sniper Four fell in behind them.

All the allied pilots were on the Blue Team. The Red Team was the Aggressor Squadron.

They flew in formation across the sky, flirting with the edges of the military zone called Area 51.

Ginger—Blue Sniper Two—couldn't help himself. "What do you think will happen if I take a picture of Area 51?"

Dex knew none of them would have bought a cell phone into the aircraft with them. No pilot did. "I think you should try it and see," he said. "But before you do, give me a message for your wife. I'm not sure we'll ever see you again. Of course, I'd be happy to look out for her myself—if you know what I mean."

Blue Two laughed. "That's a good reason not to risk a pic."

"You think?" Blue Three said. "Ironman is a beast with the ladies."

"I'd rather not think about that, thank you," Blue Two said.

Dex tuned out their chatter. He used to be a beast with the ladies, but not since the crash. He hadn't so much as chatted up a woman since the February before the crash. Until this morning, that was. He wondered where Eleanor was.

He tried to put the thought out of his head, and he realized the others were still discussing his exploits with women.

"Stop it," Dex said.

"Well, that took you long enough to shut it down," Blue Sniper Two said.

"I was thinking about something else. How about a little radio silence?" It was a good exercise; generally speaking, no one knew what kind of radios the enemy had and whether they could read their transmissions. As a rule, at Red Flag, each mission had a different frequency, so every maneuver was a surprise to the opposing force. Only the surveillance team, nearly fifty thousand feet above, had an overall picture of who was doing what.

The three pilots behind him didn't argue. All three clicked their microphones in agreement.

It took them about twenty minutes to reach the outer boundary of the bombing zone. "Keep your eyes open for the Aggressors," Dex said. "They know this area much better than we do, and they could be anywhere."

"Roger that, Ironman."

Dex swiveled his head to check for bandits. To his left there was nothing, nor above him or to his right. Maybe his team had reached the zone quicker than the Aggressor Squadron thought they would. Maybe…

"Blue Sniper Four, you are dead. Come on back to base," base command ordered.

"Shit," Blue Sniper Four said.

Adrenaline spiked through Dexter's blood. "Peel out. Peel out!" he yelled a second before banking sharply to the right. With that maneuver, he caught sight of the enemy aircraft just for a second. It ranged out of view as soon as he completed his turn. "Stay on target. I'm chasing him down."

He increased his altitude to get a better view of who had killed Blue Four and pulled above the ridge, convinced the bandit was hiding in the crags. The American aircraft were gray, exactly the same color as the rock on the ridges, making them hard to see.

So instead of looking at the rock, he checked for an aircraft shadow on the flat earth. He saw nothing. He was about to swing away to get back on target, when a glance behind him showed a shadow on the desert of an aircraft stalking him.

Damn. He dropped close to the ground. Very, very close to the ground, hoping the enemy pilot would be too chicken to follow. "Blue Sniper Two, you are dead. Come back to base," Nellis control said. Damn. There were just two of them now.

Dex swung his aircraft from side to side in an arc to avoid the flares the enemy aircraft was shooting toward him.

Safe. For the moment. He banked right again and came back over the ridge toward the bombing zone. The bandit was still on his tail, the bastard.

He dropped to the floor of the valley and taunted his pursuer by slowing and keeping straight. He took a breath and tried to imagine what the other pilot was thinking, and in the second he knew he was in range, he used his air brakes and pulled his aircraft up. The bandit sped by underneath, and the pursuer became the pursued.

He pulled his aircraft behind the Aggressor and stayed in the pilot's blind spot—six o'clock high. But the bandit banked sharply to the left and sped over the ridge.

Dex now had a decision to make: pursue or continue to the bomb range. He chose the latter. Better to hit a target and be shot down afterward than to engage in a dogfight and not find your target at all.

"Blue Sniper Three, you are dead. Return to base."

Dex took a breath. It was just him now; he had made the right decision on the target. He readied his flare missiles and accelerated toward the target. He had no time to waste, and the longer he took there, the more of a target he made himself.

The missile flare's light system in the control panel flashed blue, making it easy for him to find the button when he was ready to drop. In three seconds he could see the convoy below him, stationary and unmanned for the purposes of this exercise.

He dropped his reflective visor to block the overwhelming glare of the sun in his eyes. He just concentrated on the target.

He held his finger over the blue flashing button. Three, two...

Just as he was about to press the button, an aircraft came out of the sun directly at him. Sirens blared in the cockpit: *"Collision! Collision!"*

Instinctively he pushed his aircraft below the other aircraft and rolled to the right. He heard an enemy flare fall on top of his aircraft. Fuck. He tried to steady his heartbeat, but he couldn't. Suddenly the desert of Nevada became the desert of Iraq in his mind.

The alert system blaring in his ears, the terror, and his brain trying to work through the situation without freezing. He couldn't. He was going down. Going down.

In a second he realized the sirens had stopped. He wasn't crashing. He was flying at five hundred feet, alive.

"Blue Sniper One, you're toast. Return to base. Aggressor Squadron is victorious."

Over the RAF controller's voice, Dex could hear the whoops and hollers of the Americans in the background.

His thigh took the brunt of his frustration, as it usually did. Fuck. He ripped his mask off his face and tried to calm down.

He took a look at his small map, adjusted his bearings,

and headed back to base, reattaching his oxygen mask. The Typhoon took on some altitude to avoid the wear and tear low-level flying inflicted on the aircraft.

He couldn't fucking believe the whole team had failed in their mission. He wanted to hit someone really badly. Maybe this was why all the missions were so far away from base. It gave all "killed" pilots an opportunity to think about what they'd done wrong and calm down on their way back.

And there was no doubt they would need every minute of the forty it was going to take to get back to base. He wondered how many other teams have been thwarted by the Aggressor Squadron that morning. His team was going to have to take them down if he had any chance of getting his command back.

Fuck, he needed a drink.

CHAPTER FIVE

Y ou fucking cut me off back there," Munster's voice came over her mic, fury bubbling over the airwaves.

"I'm sorry. Did you think we were taking turns shooting at the bad guys? This isn't a movie," Eleanor replied, shaking her head.

She heard a very short burst of laughter and looked to her right. Killer, the Aggressor Squadron leader, turned to face her from the cockpit just a few meters from her wingtip.

"We are in formation for a reason," Munster said. She pictured him thumping something on his flight deck.

"Only until we reach the target. Do we need to train you again when we get on the ground?" She couldn't help herself. She could never leave him with the last word.

"Goddamn you. I'm going to kill you!" he roared.

She didn't really have a good comeback for that, so she did what she always did when she wanted to really piss him off. She opened her mic and giggled.

What came next was a barrage of bad language, anger, and shouting.

Eleanor rolled her eyes. If she had done that, exactly what Munster had just done, shouted and sworn, she'd be called unstable, maybe hormonal, and way too emotional to fly. But because he was a man, they labeled him as passionate and committed. *Should* be committed, more like. To some kind of mental institution for juvenile delinquents.

Killer cut Munster off. "Chill, dude." He was a man of few words, and Eleanor appreciated that.

"Sorry, guys, but she's reckless," Munster said.

"Daring," she countered, unable to ignore him.

"Daring? You're a danger to everyone around you," he spat.

"That shouldn't matter to you—you're never around me. You're always in my afterburn." *Just stop it. Stop talking.*

"You're going to get us all killed," he said.

"You were the only one who got killed in this mission," Killer said. "Enough now."

"That's only because my radar kept flickering on and off. Fucking avionics."

Eleanor rolled her eyes. That was 100 percent always the way. There was a certain type of pilot who returned from every failed mission blaming his equipment in some way. Because it couldn't possibly ever be pilot error. They had a world-class crew who would never let the Aggressor Squadron take off if their equipment wasn't all the way perfect.

"I'm going to tell the crew chief you blame his team's

workmanship for your epic fail today, Munster," Eleanor said.

"Just shut your mouth," he replied.

"Enough," Killer repeated.

"She started it," Munster whined.

"OMG," Eleanor said, marveling at his immaturity and countering with her own valley girl impression.

"Can it. All of you. Jesus." Poor Killer, trying to keep the peace.

She took a breath and released some of the tension in her shoulders. It was a beautiful day; she should just appreciate the opportunity to be up in the sky. She wasn't going to let Munster, the douche bag, take away the joy of her win. Instead she thought about what she was going to do that evening. She'd won. She'd neutralized the enemy, and she was going to celebrate.

But not at the mixer. Life was too short for that shit show.

She got out of her aircraft on the tarmac and waited for someone to tow it into the hangar. She removed her helmet and ran her hand through her short strands, relishing the breeze that blew through them, cooling off her helmet head.

Killer walked toward her, pulling off his own helmet. "We need to talk about you and Munster," he said.

"Yeah, I know. I feel like he's losing it," she replied, unzipping the top part of her flight suit and pulling off the shoulders. The tan-colored T-shirt she wore underneath was damp with sweat.

"No. I mean you," he said, staring at her.

"What do you mean? He's the one always crying that it's

not fair." There was no fucking way Killer was going to blame
Munster's behavior on her.

"Forget him. You're a great pilot, but no one can see that
because you're not a good team player. And you know the
military values a team player above anything else. If you can't
find a way to get along with him, then I don't have a place
for you here." He stared at her for a second. "Besides, you got
too close to that Typhoon. Coming out of the sun at him like
that." He shook his head and turned to leave.

"Are you saying it was the wrong thing to do?" she asked,
astounded.

"As long as you don't crash, it's a team win. If you crash, it's
your fault, and your fault alone," he said over his shoulder.

She was speechless, utterly speechless. She'd never really
put that together in her head before. Or maybe she had, but
her ego hadn't accepted anything other than victory over
Munster. "Are you telling him that he has to learn how to
work with me as well?"

Killer, who had always had her six, looked back at her and
shrugged. It was a stupid question, because Killer was one of
the good guys. There was no way he'd not also rip Munster a
new one.

She wanted to hurl her helmet at the ground, or her aircraft, or at Munster's head. She had to get out of there; she
needed a break. She had packed only one dress with her, and
she was going to use it tonight. She needed to take her mind
off everything.

She also needed to end her eight-year dry spell. Although
judging by her luck recently, she wasn't holding her breath.

Eleanor left the dorm area, having showered and almost de-
fiantly slipping into her one dress and covering it up with a
black leather jacket. Before she left, though, she took one last
walk down to the hangars. Sometimes she just felt the need
to be with her aircraft. To look it over, to reassure herself that
they were a team.

She strode along the flight line, smiling to herself as the
last planes landed in the desert dusk. The night sky was
layered with orange clouds as the final rays of the sun disappeared. As she walked alongside the hangars, the taxiway
lights lit up, flooding the tarmac with pools of light. She
took a deep breath of cooler night air.

A few people were still on the other side of the airfield.
She heard a strain of music floating on the breeze. She
rolled her eyes. That would be the Australians garnering
their first noise complaint of Red Flag. Not the last,
though, probably.

As she reached the hangar door, she noticed Missy walking the flight line behind her. Missy "Warbird" Malden, was
an F-15 Strike Eagle weapons officer. She took the backseat
to her pilot Francis "Freak" Conrad, who was rarely anywhere he was supposed to be.

She raised her hand as a greeting and yanked the hangar
door to get in. The door wouldn't open. She put her shoulder
into it and tried to push and then tried to wiggle it free. But
the door wouldn't shift. She stood back, fists at her waist,
considering the best method of attack.

"Yeah, it's not going to open," Missy said, standing at the

center of the twenty-foot door and looking from one end to the other.

"What do you mean?" Eleanor asked.

"There's a big-ass padlock on the other side," Missy told her.

"Fucker." Eleanor strode toward the other side of the door. "Since when have they locked these hangars?"

"Never," Missy said, catching up with her. "But I'm all about it if it means we don't have to sleep with the planes."

Eleanor grunted at her. That was the truth. Since one country, who shall remain unnamed, broke into all the hangars to take photos of every country's military equipment, pilots and crew had taken it upon themselves to sleep in the hangar to guard the aircraft and equipment. It was half a precaution, half team building. But everyone knew that while taking photos was one thing, letting someone into the hangar so they could sabotage your aircraft was something completely different. And that's why nobody really complained about those nights they had to sleep in the hangar instead of partying in Las Vegas.

She squatted next to what looked like a padlock, took off her sunglasses, and squinted at it. "Well what the fuck is that?"

Missy crouched next to her. "Beats me."

The thing keeping the doors shut looked like a little computer, almost like a tablet. It had an antenna at the back and a thick steel cable.

"There's no way the military paid for a high-tech lock when we can't even persuade them to issue us padlocks," Missy said.

"I really don't like this. I don't like not being able to get to my aircraft." Eleanor stood and looked down the flight line at the hangars to the right and the left of her. "Who's that?"

A man in a U.S. Air Force uniform drove toward them in a golf cart. "Since when do we have golf carts at Nellis?" Eleanor asked.

"Look. He's stopping at every hangar. He's taking off these"—she gestured at the lock—"things, whatever they are." Missy frowned and squinted at the guy.

"Wait, what? He's turning around. Hey! Hey you!" she shouted, waving both arms over her head before realizing that raised her dress length by about five inches. She dropped them fast.

The airman on the golf cart hesitated, as if torn. After a couple of seconds, he executed a slow wide loop and trundled back to them. "Yes, Major?" he said, looking at Missy, who was still in her uniform.

"Take ours off," Eleanor said.

"Can't do that, ma'am," he said, his eyes gazing out over the empty runway, as if there was something fascinating happening.

"I'm telling you to open the hangar," Eleanor said. What the fuck was going on here? No one stopped a pilot from going into a hangar. Ever.

"Ma'am, I have this radio, see? I get to go up and down the tarmac, opening the hangars as they tell me to." He put the radio back in the cup holder.

"Who did you get your orders from?" Missy said, pulling out her phone.

The airman smiled. It looked pretty smug to Eleanor. "General Daniels," he said, as if they were two separate sentences.

Eleanor closed her eyes for a second and casually stepped to the side so the airman wouldn't recognize her. Being the general's daughter was bad enough, but having her father get one over on her in public was unbearable.

She wanted to scream. The one time she had a shot to prove that it was her skill that had got her to where she was, and not her father's influence, and he fucked it all up by deciding to grace Red Flag with his presence for the first time. Anger spiked in her. Could she do one thing without him interfering? "Okay, Sergeant, you can go. No, wait. Will those locks be made available to us during the competition?"

"I don't know. I doubt it. I've been told to repackage them in boxes after I've collected them. They belong to TGO."

What was TechGen-One doing locking their hangars? Maybe they were testing out the locks? Sometimes they did that—testing out small bits of equipment before selling them to the military. But they could test them out on any door in the world. Why do it at Red Flag? Eleanor shrugged and turned back to Missy, who was holding her phone to her ear.

"Conrad. Get over here. They've locked our hangar. We can't get in," Missy said into the phone. She shook her head as she listened to his reply. "Goddammit, just put the woman down and come do your job."

Eleanor turned away so Missy wouldn't see her smile.

Conrad had a reputation. Great pilot, great friend, terrible ladies' man.

"Oh, she's a *gymnast*. Well that's okay then," Missy said, nudging her.

When Eleanor looked back at her, Missy put a finger gun under her own chin and pulled the trigger, simultaneously rolling her eyes and shaking her head. Poor woman—she'd had four years of Conrad's exploits.

"No. We are taking tomorrow's night shift in the hangar." There was a pause. "When they remove the locks on the hangar, they're taking them away. We still have to take a shift." Another pause as Conrad obviously gave her some excuse. "Kill me now," Missy said. "Get your ass back to base." She hung up on him.

"I have no idea how you put up with him," Eleanor said. One more reason Eleanor was thankful that she flew solo. In her F-16 Viper, she was in charge of everything.

"It's getting harder. He seems to be getting worse." Missy nodded toward two metal folding chairs on the ground, half covered in sand and dirt. Eleanor fell into place next to her.

They picked them up and positioned them slap bang in front of the hangar doors. They were going to see who was inside and what they were doing. Because no one fucked with her plane without her knowing about it.

Once they'd sat down, Eleanor started again. "What do you mean he's getting worse?"

"A new woman every night, virtually at least. It's hard to imagine there are enough girls in any town." Missy sighed. "His attention is slipping. I don't mean in the cockpit, of course. But everything outside just seems to be a haze to him. He goes from his aircraft into a haze, then finds a woman, and after that he's back in a haze until he sits in his aircraft again."

"You want me to talk to him?" Eleanor wondered if he would talk to her, a fellow pilot.

"God no. I speak to him about it all the time. He just denies it. Anyway, I've been thinking about getting a transfer, so it's not like he'll be my problem for much longer."

Eleanor fought against sounding shocked. "Well he'll definitely miss you then." It was pretty unusual for a weapons officer to ask to separate from her pilot. Things must really be bad. Poor Missy. Poor Conrad, come to that. He'd never find another weapons officer as good as Missy.

"Enough about my boring life. Tell me about your boring life," Missy said with a grin.

Eleanor laughed. And then laughed a little more. "You laugh because if you don't, you'll cry."

"Please tell me you're not in a dry spell still. I don't think I even knew you when you weren't having a dry spell." Missy stroked Eleanor's shoulder as if she were stroking a child's hair.

"You're a fine one to talk." She shrugged Missy's hand off.

Missy sat back in her chair stretched out her legs and put her hands behind her head. "Yeah, but I'm celibate for a reason. Two reasons. Firstly I'm trying to set a good example for Conrad, and secondly he's put me off all men."

"Not all men are like Conrad," Eleanor said. She hoped.

"So what's your excuse then?" Missy asked.

"Oh God. Who has time? And you know what happens if you sleep with someone in uniform. Nothing is ever a secret. And that's all it takes. One night, and then they talk about you forever." It was true. It was a risk she couldn't take. Unfortunately, for women, sex took on a whole new meaning in the military. And she already had it hard with people assuming she got her rank because of her father. She didn't want to give anyone any reason to suggest she'd slept with someone for rank.

"It sucks to be us," Missy said. As she spoke, the door of the hangar beeped. No, it wasn't the door of the hangar; it was the lock. It beeped, and the hangar door started rolling open. Both Missy and Eleanor leaned forward in their chairs.

"No, it sucks to be him." Eleanor nodded toward a man pushing the door open. He wasn't military; that was for sure. At least, he was in civvies and his hair was way longer than military length.

Eleanor got up. "Who are you?"

He ignored her and continued to push the door open. Two men drove out of the hangar in a golf cart, and as they passed the door, he jumped onto the back and they rolled off down the flight line without a word.

Eleanor's jaw dropped open. "What the fuck just happened?"

Missy ran into the hangar. "They had a vehicle in here. How would we know if they dinged one of our aircraft?" The smallest undetected dent could cause the airframe to buckle in flight.

"Don't touch anything." Eleanor knew there was only one

thing to do. Because the possibility that something had happened to the aircraft, and one of them may crash, trumped her desire to stay way out of contact with her father. She dialed his number.

"Good evening, Eleanor," her father said.

"There were people in our hangar. Civilians. They had a golf cart in there. Do you know anything about it? Can you call security? The aircraft are stacked in there. There's no way they didn't hit something." Under normal circumstances, she would have gone straight to base security; however, since her father had given orders to a mere sergeant about those weird locks, she wanted to gauge his involvement before she did so.

"Don't fuss so, Eleanor. Why don't you come to my office before you cause everyone else to panic?" It annoyed her that he sounded amused.

"I'm here with Missy Malden. She saw them too."

He hesitated for a few beats and then said, "Just come to my office." He hung up.

He had an office here? Since he was probably the only general on the base, she figured he would be easy to find. She sighed and stuffed her phone back in her jacket.

"Going to see daddy dearest?" Missy's face twisted into a sympathetic smile.

Eleanor puffed air from her cheeks. "I guess so."

"Luck," Missy said.

Eleanor nodded. "Thanks." She couldn't help but think that if her father was at all involved in whatever had been going on in the hangar, Eleanor was screwed.

After a few false starts—and forget the embarrassment

from having to ask strangers where your own father's office was—she found the building he was using.

Outside her father's office, she paced in front of his executive assistant, Captain Wilks, mainly because she knew he couldn't concentrate on his work when she—or anyone—was in his peripheral vision. It was childish, but it was habit. She barely noticed herself doing it. She couldn't stop thinking about what the civilians had been doing in her hangar with no supervision. How could any of the pilots get in their aircraft with any confidence?

She'd woken up that morning so full of hope and excitement. Just wanting to prove her worth to her team. But in the space of a day, she'd discovered her father had elbowed himself into Red Flag—the one time she thought she could prove herself without him being around—she'd been bawled out by Killer, and now she found that her aircraft could have been compromised.

Nothing about this was good for her. And although she knew tears would never come out of her eyes, everything inside her was telling her to curl up in a corner and cry her eyes out. How could everything have gone so wrong in one day?

She was so deep in her thoughts that she hadn't realized she was less pacing the office than stomping up and down it.

Wilks threw down his pen and folded his arms, leaned back in his chair, and just watched her with an "un-fucking-believable" expression on his face. She glared at him for a second and then ignored him.

He got up and left.

With nobody left to irritate, she threw herself onto the sofa outside her father's office and put her head in her hands. She was trying to figure out a way to test the aircraft, wondering how long it would take the crew to check and double-check all the aircraft in the hangar.

Her head jerked up when she heard loud voices coming from her father's office. She strained to hear what they were saying but could only make out the odd word. Nothing made sense anyway. Deep down in her heart, she wondered for a second if he was reaming out the person who allowed people in her hangar. That maybe he was angry on her behalf. Maybe he was worried for her safety. But the rational part of her brain knew that wasn't true. There was a deep irony that people thought he had anything to do with her progression in the air force. He'd barely even noticed that she existed for the vast majority of her life. And when he did, he treated her more like a vague acquaintance.

The voices started to become clearer, and she figured whoever was in the office was moving toward the door.

"Share prices will rocket," a voice said. "This will be good for all of us."

Eleanor strained to hear more.

"And this is clean?" her father replied.

"Totally. It's sanitized, protecting both you and me." The other person laughed, reassuring. "It's going to make you millions. It's going to make our friends in high places billions. Just don't rock the boat at this late stage. Do you understand?"

"What about the hangars?" her father asked.

Eleanor jumped up, a chill rushing down her spine. What were they talking about?

"We pay you the big bucks to manage situations like this. Why do you think we had you assigned here?"

What?

The door popped open and she stumbled backward, only just realizing that she had virtually put her ear to the door.

Her father and TechGen-One CEO Gerald Danvers stared at her.

Shit.

"How long were you standing there?" Danvers asked. Her father stayed silent, but his stricken look shocked her.

"I just got here. I was trying to hear if you were alone in there," Eleanor said, with a bright smile that did nothing to alter her father's expression.

Both men just stared at her for a second. Her father looked like he wasn't seeing her but was running through thousands of options in his brain. Danvers's face remained impassive. But without saying anything, he turned to her father and stared at him for a long couple of seconds. Her father didn't meet his eyes.

She suddenly had the feeling she was in the wrong place at the wrong time with the wrong people. Not a totally alien feeling, but one that left her more scared than usual.

She stuck out her hand and smiled, hoping the smile looked normal and not manic. "Good to see you again. The Aggressor Squadron was victorious today," she babbled. "We had a good mission." She continued to smile, but even she could tell she was showing panic.

The man shook her hand. "Always good to see a victorious pilot. So much better than…" His voice trailed off and his eyes flickered to her father. "Than the alternative."

As he held her hand, she looked at her father. His eyes were closed, as if he'd just witnessed something awful.

Danvers left the office, and her father stood back silently to allow her in. She hesitated, but he stood in silence, forcing her to acquiesce. He shut the door behind him. "How much did you really hear?" His voice was low.

"Everything from the fact that the share price will rocket." Eleanor put her hands on her hips, suddenly feeling braver now that it was just her and her father in the room. "Wait. *What* has been sanitized?"

A vein pulsed in her father's neck, and she realized she'd pushed him too far. "How dare you, Eleanor. My private conversations are nothing to do with you. And that you make it clear that you were eavesdropping on a private conversation—in front of the other party to the conversation, no less—is inconceivable. Now leave. Your aircraft is fine. You interrupted a routine security sweep."

Eleanor shook her head at her father's words. "What about the millions? How about telling me exactly how a private contractor can have a three-star general 'assigned' to Red Flag?"

"Goddamn it, Eleanor!" her father shouted, slamming his fist on the desk in front of him. "TechGen-One isn't just a contractor. Their shareholders are congressmen, senators, cabinet members." He was so enraged, saliva gathered at the corners of his mouth.

Terror spiked through her. She'd never seen her father lose control. Never seen the fear in his eyes that she was looking at now. Never been scared of him before.

She held her hands up in surrender. "It's okay," she said soothingly. "Forget I asked."

"You must not talk about this to anyone. You hear? Not a soul. It's life or death." Panic rose in his voice again.

"I promise." She backed out of the room, wanting to un-hear and unsee everything from the last ten minutes.

He watched her go.

She shut the office door quietly and rested her forehead on it, her mind racing. What had just happened? What was her father involved in? What was TechGen-One involved in?

As she made her way back outside, a man slammed into her shoulder. "Sorry," she said absently. The man stopped, and she looked at him. He was the man with long hair she'd seen coming out of her hangar. She opened her mouth to say something, but his expression stopped her.

He just stared at her, chewing on a toothpick. He slowly looked her up and down, and then turned to leave, heading toward her father's office. She watched him go.

He didn't turn back.

CHAPTER SIX

Eleanor contemplated going back to the dorm, but she didn't want to talk to anyone—especially Missy, who knew she'd been going to see her father and would want to know what the men had been doing in their hangar. She opted for her first plan: hide in a bar downtown for a while.

As she left base in one of the taxis that perpetually loitered in front of the welcome center, she noticed that the security checkpoints, usually manned by active duty airmen, had been replaced by TechGen-One employees. It wasn't unheard of; some of the other military bases, both in the United States and overseas, were secured by private contractors. She'd just never seen that at Nellis, and it did nothing to ease her pumping fear.

TGO could order her father to attend Red Flag, they had complete authority over the hangars and aircraft, and they were in charge of security.

Thirty minutes previously she would have told anyone

who asked that it was great that the contractor had paid for Red Flag, that she couldn't begin to imagine the cost of it, that she was thankful Red Flag hadn't been canceled. But now she realized TGO must be getting something huge in return. Something that involved her father. Something that involved billions of dollars and the complicity of lobbyists and people high up in the government. She just couldn't figure out what.

It was something big enough to scare her father. And she had never known anything to scare her father. Ever.

She clenched her fists and then shook them, trying to get her blood circulating. Who could she go to with this? Her father was the ranking officer on base, the military police had been taken over by TGO personnel, and she wasn't 100 percent sure what "this" was.

She got dropped off a couple of blocks from the strip; the new layout had made it impossible to get out of any taxi on the main part of the strip. It had probably meant fewer drunken fatalities as well.

The mixer that evening was in one of the private meeting rooms at the Paris casino. The bar Eleanor was heading to was two blocks behind it. She didn't mind walking, even in high heels. And even though it would have been quicker to walk through the casino floor, she was taking the long way in case she got shanghaied and dragged into the party. She needed time alone to process what had happened, because otherwise she'd be flying tomorrow with it in her head.

She'd gone to the mixer the first time she'd been a Red Flag, and that one time was enough. It had been forced and uncomfortable. Lower-ranking people virtually genuflecting to the higher-ranking officers. The expectation was all the different nationalities would socialize and become friends. But that wasn't easy when you'd shot them down that very day. Not that they would necessarily know it was you who'd shot them down, but it was still awkward. No one really wanted to be there, but to the big cheeses, it was important to say the different countries had fully integrated and were friendly colleagues. Mostly, though, the pilots who went, even if they weren't forced to, were kiss asses.

She picked up her pace toward the crosswalk to see if she could get across while the little green man was flashing. She ground to a halt when she realized there was no way she would make it. Just as she was reaching for the button, a blow to her shoulder launched her into oncoming traffic.

A tourist limo screeched to a halt—a mere two inches from her hip.

"Get out of the road, lady!" the driver yelled out his window. "Stop drinking and go home."

She held up her hands to him as she stumbled out of the road and back to the sidewalk. She looked around, but no one was there who could have shoved her. Jesus, she could have been killed.

"I fucking hate Vegas," the driver said as he pulled off.

She just stood on the sidewalk, unable to fathom what had just happened. She'd forgotten how awful tourists were. Someone had pretty near killed her with their carelessness, then just walked off like nothing had happened.

She needed a drink. She waited for the walk signal,

checked both directions, and strode across the intersection, rolling her shoulder to ease the pain. God, what had he bumped into her with? A steel bat?

Las Vegas was definitely dangerous for her health.

It had taken her a few minutes to get to an intersection where she could actually cross. These strip improvements really took the fun out of walking in Vegas. High fences and steep curbs meant that the strip was essentially a highway for traffic. She couldn't be bothered to fight against the flow of tourists on the huge bridge that linked Planet Hollywood and CityCenter, which is why she usually skirted those areas.

It was a pain in the ass to get to her favorite bar, Bipartisan Measures. From Nellis you either paid an extra $10 to cross the strip, or you had to walk an extra half mile. But Bipartisan Measures was the only place she felt comfortable. It was an exact replica of the original bar in Washington, D.C., where she'd lived most of her life.

She'd first gone to the bar with her father. He used to take confidential meetings, the high, curtained booths providing cover for people he wasn't supposed to be seen with. Those curtained booths had also been the scene of her first sexual experience, with the son of an army brigadier general. Fake IDs, Southern Comfort and Diet Coke, and a boy who knew what he was doing.

Now that she thought about it, she wondered what her father had been doing in a place like that and who he'd been meeting with. And if any of that had any relation to what was going on now. All she remembered was an endless parade of men in suits and coloring books she was given to play with as she sat in the corner.

She was deep in thought when she felt a hand on her shoulder. She jumped and turned, automatically grabbing the wrist of her assailant.

"Easy, tiger," the man said. She did a double take and dropped his wrist. It was the TGO guy again. She backed away from him, fight or flight battling for supremacy. "These limo drivers…Am I right?" He tutted and shook his head as if in dismay. His toothpick bobbed in his mouth.

Suddenly, without actually thinking it, she knew he was the one who had pushed her into traffic.

Outrage overpowered fear, stupidly. "What are you doing?"

"Keep walking. We just want to talk," the man said, nodding in the direction she had been walking.

"I'm not walking anywhere with you." She looked around for someone to appeal to, but this was Vegas. No one looked you in the eye, and everyone was suspicious of being scammed in one way or another.

He smiled. "Walk with me, or I'll be looking for your father next."

Her mind whirled. What did he mean? He'd just been in her father's office.

"He told me what you'd overheard, and he told me what he'd accidentally spilled about the company I work for. If we felt there was a security threat, we'd have to take action. You understand that, right?"

"Security threat? I can virtually guarantee that I have a

higher security clearance than you." She was playing for time. Trying to get her head around what was happening to her. And to her father.

He smiled again and nodded down the road, holding a hand out to allow her to go first.

Hesitantly, she continued to walk. She was concerned that he had said "*we* just want to talk." Her eyes took in everyone around her, looking for the "we"—the tourists, the workers—and then she found them. Two other men who weren't looking at her but looking at the man who was walking with her. Were they waiting for his orders?

Fear threaded through her, but what could they really do here? In front of everyone? Plus, Vegas had more cameras in the street than nearly any other city in the United States.

"What do you want to talk about?" she asked, trying to inject more anger into her voice than she felt. She didn't want him to know how scared she was.

"I just want to be sure that we can rely on your discretion. The conversation you overheard was classified." he said. "That's all. Just usual, run-of-the-mill security issues. We're just crossing our t's and dotting our—"

"What conversation?" Maybe if he told her, she'd be able to figure out if her father had really just thrown her under the bus—or limo if she thought about it literally—or if he'd fobbed this guy off with a lie.

"You know which conversation. If you make me repeat it, it won't be confidential and then we'll all be in trouble. If you say anything to anybody, your father will be in big trouble. And if your father is fired or imprisoned, or should have a tragic accident, what do you think will happen to you? So, I'm saying it would be best for everyone if you just forgot everything."

"I have quite a good memory. So does my father. How do you think he'll react when I tell him you shoved me in front of traffic?" *Go on. Admit it, you fucker.*

"Do you really want to find out who he sides with?"

He hadn't denied it.

She opened her mouth to speak, but he grabbed her by the arm, his fingers like pincers. He smiled, and to passersby they would have looked as if they were discussing which restaurant to go to. "This is way beyond your pay grade. And the farther up you go, the messier it gets. And by messier, I mean more painful. Just keep your mouth shut, and everything will be fine."

She wrenched her arm away from him. "Leave me alone. Leave my father alone."

He smiled, a perfect white-toothed Hollywood smile. "Don't make me come find you again. If I think you're noncompliant"—he brushed his hands down her bare arms as if he were sweeping dust from the shoulders of a child—"I'll be forced to—"

Fear and fury wrapped themselves around each other. Heat rushed through her, and she put her hands on his shoulders and kneed him in the balls. His torso caved with the pain, and although he didn't fall to the ground, he bent far enough down that with her hands still on his shoulders, she could lean into his ear. "Just checking to see if you've got any."

Before he could reply, or his goons could intercept her, she darted away. As soon as she put a few groups of tourists between them, she whipped off her high heels and ran into the nearest casino. Paris. She went through the doors, pasted a smile on her face, and weaved her way through the throngs surrounding the tables. She rounded a pillar and stopped to catch her breath and put her shoes back on.

What the hell was her father into?

One of the blackjack dealers was looking at her in between dealing to the players at his table. He looked concerned. For a second she wondered how she appeared; it wasn't as if she'd been in an actual fight. She ran her fingers through her hair, brushed her sundress down, and, convinced she looked okay, sent a bright smile his way.

She stepped out from behind the pillar and glanced behind her toward the doors she had fled through. Everything looked normal. Maybe they hadn't seen her come in. Maybe she'd kneed him hard enough that they'd have to go to the hospital. She sighed and closed her eyes for a second in relief. She turned to make her way to one of the side exits, near the conference rooms, and then she saw them. Not Mr. Hollywood himself, but his two henchmen, weaving their way through the casino scanning all the tables and all the patrons. One of them had a phone to his ear.

As her brain tried to filter out the panic, she suddenly realized where she was: the Paris. And if her estimations were right, an hour into the dreaded mixer. She would be safe there.

She tried to remember the room it was in. Something to do with an aircraft. She slowed down to look at the meeting board display. Concorde. The Concorde Ballroom.

At the end of the corridor—fucking perfect. Especially since she was back in her heels. There was one man moving behind her, which meant the other was trying to head her off somehow. The ballroom was in sight—just a few more paces. She took one last look back at the man chasing her, as if in slow motion. His face had hate etched all over it, and she had no idea why. Unless it was just the fact that she'd kneed his boss in the nuts. She kicked up to a run and burst through the doors, just as he reached out to grab her.

The doors swung open loudly, banging against the wall behind it. About fifty people looked around, including some high-ranking officers from Nellis. The door closed behind her, and she took a breath of relief. "I was so worried that I would be late," she said to the people staring aghast at her inelegant and loud entrance.

They turned back to their conversations, thank God.

Great. She would have to stay awhile and make sure she left with someone. The room was packed, way over a thousand people. Senior officers, pilots, crew—she looked at the bar—and some local girls looking for some action. They were in the right place.

She fought her way to the bar, badly needing a drink, even though she had intended on staying dry so she would be in good shape for the next day's mission. That was not going to happen now.

She ordered a white wine, thinking that would be better than hard liquor, and took a sip of the unfortunately room-temperature Chardonnay. Her nerves were still shot; she didn't want to look around her in case she saw someone she knew. How could she possibly make small talk after what had happened? How could she go back on base? Fly tomorrow?

Mr. Hollywood had been right, though. Her career, like it or not, was inextricably linked to her father's. He had told her that himself a million times. Even though she had earned every rank and every accolade by herself, precious few people believed it. This was supposed to be the one place where she could prove her worth without her father's influence. But he even managed to fuck that over for her.

She took another shaky gulp of wine, then placed her palms down on the bar to try to steady her hands. Her body just wouldn't accept that she wasn't in danger anymore. She could almost feel her organs quivering. She closed her eyes and pictured herself soaring through cumulus clouds into the blue sky, the faint rattle of a thermal jostling her aircraft. She took a breath and then another breath.

Just as she was beginning to feel normal, a hand clapped down on her shoulder. Fear pierced her happy place. She spun and punched the owner of the hand in the face.

Shit. The man reeled backward, holding both hands to his nose. A hush came over the bar crowd. "Are you fucking kidding me?" Munster spat from beneath his hands.

Horror washed over her. She reached out a hand in aid. "Oh God. I'm sorry. I didn't—"

"You saw that, right? You saw that? Bitch hit me," Munster said, wildly looking around at the people at the bar.

No one said anything. Thankfully, no one else in the room

had noticed. But that seemed to infuriate Munster more. "That's it. You're done here."

His nose was bleeding, and she turned to the bar to grab some napkins. She held them out to him, but he clenched his fist and whacked it down on her forearm. Napkins fluttered all over the floor. The pain was excruciating, and she wondered if he had broken her ulna. She held her arm with her other hand. "Are you kidding me? Did you just try to break my arm?" she ground out between clenched teeth.

"You just broke my nose, so I can do whatever the fuck I want now. It's over for you. Everyone saw it."

She looked around, found everyone had slowly moved away from them. She turned to look at the barman, who just shrugged. "Everyone?" she asked.

He looked around too. There were definitely people watching, but mostly the crew. She didn't recognize any of them.

"Look. Let's just leave it, walk away and pretend this never happened," she said, mustering up a conciliatory tone.

"No way. No fucking way. You are out of here—and I'm going make sure of it. I mean Jesus, Daniels, what did you expect? You join my squadron, and you get promoted almost immediately, thanks to your daddy. And then you think you can take the commander spot when Killer retires? I'm not gonna let that happen. And now the only way you can keep your position is to start fucking the three-star generals here tonight, bitch." He was shouting by the end.

Her left fist was flying toward his face before he had finished his sentence.

CHAPTER SEVEN

Dex Stone was sucking up the absolute worst part of the Red Flag exercise. He checked his watch—good, he'd be out of there in less than an hour. This "mixer" was anything but. All the teams kept to themselves, worried that an inopportune comment under the influence of a little alcohol could cost them victory, or at least bragging rights.

Nursing his mineral water—cunningly decorated with lime to look like a cocktail—he checked out the competition. Although on the face of it, it was hard to tell who were the competing pilots, who were the crew, and who were the civilians.

The group of guys in a booth sharing bottles of red wine had to be the French team. They were well known for doing whatever it took to win; he committed their faces to his memory. They'd been known to dig deep and play dirty for a competitive advantage. He admired that. He wondered if Jean-Luc was here. He'd bonded with the French pilot a few years back when they'd all lost—once again—to the U.S. Aggressor Squadron. The French weren't under the same orders as the RAF was: participate, collaborate, and bring home the victory. Their MO was "Do whatever it takes."

The Germans looked morosely at the Bud Light the Belgians had sent over, and Dex couldn't help but grin. One of the German pilots recognized Dex and gave an almost imperceptible nod. He lifted his glass a few millimeters in response.

They'd fought wing by wing, but now that they were away from combat, everyone was looking to their own team to take home victory.

This was the year the Aggressor Squadron was going down. At least, if he had anything to do with it. Not that today's performance was a great start. But tomorrow would be different. Tomorrow he wouldn't be a good boy and only go for the target. Tomorrow he was going on the offensive. He was going to get that bastard who'd shot him down.

He sighed and sat back in his seat. The rest of his team was having a fast meal at the chow hall and getting an early night, and he wished with all his heart that he'd stayed with them. But someone had to represent the RAF, and as the de facto leader, he felt it was his duty to put in an appearance.

A tall woman with short blond hair stood at the bar, hands placed on the steel countertop. She looked as if she was garnering courage to chat someone up. She took some deep chugs of wine and wobbled on impossibly high heels, as if a little drunk. Typical local. Looking to score with the pilots. Very *An Officer and a Gentleman*—he guessed it never got old.

He took another sip of his water. Just as long as all the others were drinking, he already had an advantage for tomorrow, and that was fine with him.

His phone entertained him for a few minutes while he read an inexplicable email chain that seemed to have originated from some poor bastard of an airman back in England who'd hit "Reply all" in error.

"Bitch!" a man shouted.

His head shot up. A guy was addressing the blonde at the bar. He looked to be military judging by his hair. Before Dex was halfway out of his seat, the woman had punched the guy clear in the nose. Dex winced but headed toward them.

"What's going on?" he asked, pushing his way to the bar.

"Bitch is crazy is what happened," the injured guy said, stuffing napkins up his nose.

"I heard you insult her, so I don't have much sympathy for you right now," he said, trying to inject some calm into the proceedings.

"Fuck off. I'm out of here. But you—I'm going to fuck you over as soon as I get the opportunity, crazy bitch."

The woman surged forward again, fury—and interestingly, fear—in her eyes. She looked familiar. Had he flown with her at some previous Red Flag?

Dex got between them. "Let it go. Come on. Looks like he's already worse off than you. Let calmer heads prevail." His whole body was tight with the innate desire to wade in and fucking fight someone. The urge wasn't unusual.

"Calmer heads? You arrogant dick." She grabbed her wine from the bar and hurled it over him.

Awesome. "Well on that note, I think I'll go. It's been a real pleasure." He walked out the same way the angry guy had, just to make sure he wasn't planning some kind of immediate retribution. He paused as the casino noises struck him—the bar was tucked away in the meeting room area, somewhat hidden from the rest of the casino floor, which is why it was a favorite for private events.

He couldn't see any sign of the guy who'd been punched, so he turned and made his way to the nearest exit. Someone bumped him as they rushed past. "Don't mind me," he said to the angry woman's back as she rushed toward the exit.

Who was she, and why was she so familiar?

Eleanor couldn't believe what had just happened. It was still early, and yet her whole evening, and probably professional life, was already in the toilet.

She pushed past people, just needing to get away from the mixer. But as soon as the casino noises started to overwhelm her, she stopped dead. Where could she go? Her breath came in unnatural gasps, as if she'd run a marathon.

This day. She wished she could just turn back the dial, start it all over again. Remake all her decisions. Or stay in bed.

Join the Peace Corps, maybe.

She just wanted to get out of there. She made an abrupt 180 turn and walked straight into a man.

"Don't mind me," he said under his breath.

She spun around and glared, her eyes sliding to scan the people walking through the corridor behind him. She was about to walk away, making the right decision not to have one more confrontation before she got to bed, when she saw one of Mr. Hollywood's goons. They locked eyes, and as soon as they did, he started making his way toward her.

Blindly, she turned toward the man she had just pissed off. "I'm so sorry." She smiled desperately. "Why don't you let me buy you a drink to apologize? Come on," she said, barely waiting for him to answer before grabbing his hand and pulling him toward the exit.

"Excuse me. Come on where?" He resisted her efforts to propel him toward the doors.

"Let's get out of here," she said, a hopeful smile on her face.

He mirrored her smile, but his was a lot more smug. "You don't remember me, do you?"

She frowned. She did know him. In a tenth of a second she clocked him. Ironman. "Sure I do. You're the guy from the bus this morning. You smell of wine. What's up with that?" She tried to tug him again, holding his hand.

"I can't imagine why," he deadpanned, still refusing to move.

She glanced over her shoulder. Goon number two was almost on top of them.

"Please," she begged, not even trying to hide her desperation now. Before he could answer, her pursuer grabbed her arm and pulled the pilot's hand from hers.

"Sorry, ma'am, you've got to come with us now," he said, still holding her arm.

"Why?" the British guy asked.

Eleanor tried to yank her arm away, but her captor held on so firmly she winced.

"Okay, that makes it easy." The Brit grabbed the man's arm away from Eleanor and spun him around, so his arm was up his back. "You should go now."

"Sure, sure, sure," the man said apologetically. Ironman let him go, but as soon as he did, the goon took a swing him.

The Brit took the punch to the jaw and staggered back a little. Then their assailant turned to her, and she punched him in his side. Unfortunately, the blow Munster had given her arm took the force out of her strike, and the guy just smiled at her. He opened his mouth to say something, and a fist came out of nowhere and landed on the side of his head. He crumpled like a napkin.

They both looked down at him and then at each other. "Wow," she said.

"Why does everyone hate you so much?" he asked.

She was about to answer when another scary-looking guy came running around the corner. "Well, you could ask him, but I suggest we run instead." She nodded toward the approaching thug.

"Jesus." He held his hand out to her, and she took it. They ran for the exit at the end of the foyer and hurried out into the arid night air.

"This way," Eleanor said. She dared not go back to the front of the hotel, where the minivans were waiting to take them back to base, so she decided to head around the back, conveniently in the direction of Bipartisan Measures.

"Drink?" she asked. It was the least she could do.

As they ran, he opened and closed his fist. "And some ice."

"Deal." At least they would be safe at the bar; everyone knew her there and would look out for her. *Them*. After *them*. Like it not, she owed this guy.

"Where are we going?" he asked.

"I know a place," she said simply.

"How far is it?" They started to slow down.

She stopped and smiled. "Do you need to take a knee?"

"Fuck off."

She deserved that.

"So, do you need to be somewhere else?" she asked.

"Anywhere but here."

She deserved that too.

CHAPTER EIGHT

What Dex really needed was to be back at the dorm reviewing last year's missions. He needed to get a good night's sleep. Fuck. He hoped his hand injury wouldn't affect his performance tomorrow. Basically, he needed to be anywhere except here right now. Dealing with the crazy woman from this morning. The crazy, beautiful woman with the smart mouth.

They both stood there, saying nothing. "Do you think we've lost them?" he asked, looking down the street.

Eleanor followed his gaze. There were only a few people on the street, and none of them looked as if they were coming after them.

"I guess so." She nodded slowly. "Thank you for helping me."

"Who were those guys? And why did they want you to go with them?" he asked.

She shook her head. "I don't…I don't know exactly."

"I find that very difficult to believe. You must have pissed them off somehow." He raised his eyebrows.

"Wow. Way to victim-blame," she said, a touch of anger flushing the words.

He stepped back a little. "Okaaay…," he said. "You're not going to hit me, are you?"

"Not unless you piss me off." She took off again walking, unnaturally quickly on her high heels.

"I'm beginning to think it may be fairly easy to piss you off," he said as she ran across the road with him in tow.

"Now, that's not a very nice thing to say," she said as she stopped on the sidewalk in front of a line of people.

"You seem to have forgotten I just watched you break a man's nose."

"I just watched you do the same," she said.

"I only did that because of you, and whatever shit storm you managed to yank me into. But let's not forget you also threw a glass of wine at me," he said.

"That's right, I did, didn't I. You owe me at least half a glass of wine, too, then." She crossed her arms defensively.

He looked up at the building. "Even if I agreed with that premise, which I don't, this bar doesn't look open." What were all these people doing lining up outside an obviously closed bar?

"It's only closed if you don't know about it. You have to be a member," she said, holding out her hand for his.

He hesitated. He should go back to base. Get away from whatever madness was following Eleanor around town. But then again, could he leave her in good conscience when she had people trying to kidnap her?

"You better give me some answers," he said, eyeing her hand.

"I promise I will," she replied, again holding her hand out. He breathed deeply and took it.

He shook his head at the triumphant smile that flashed across her face.

She drew him toward the closed door. She looked up at a camera, and the right-hand side door opened with an electronic clunk. He hesitated. What was he getting himself into?

"Just promise me you're not a spy," he said as they stepped inside.

She took both his hands in hers and pulled them up and clasped them as if she was saying a prayer. "I absolutely swear I am not a spy. Well, almost absolutely swear." She turned her back on him and walked a few paces, throwing a grin back at him over her shoulder.

"Wait a minute. Your fingers are crossed behind your back," he said, jogging a couple of steps to keep up with her in the dimly lit foyer. There were stairs leading up to an open galleried floor.

"Tell me the truth now," she said with a smile. "You don't really mind that I'm a spy, do you? I mean, you're still here."

"I am still here. But I think that might just be to keep you out of trouble. But I absolutely swear I won't tell you any secrets," he said, fighting to keep a smile from his face.

She walked up a few steps and then turned and looked down at him. "Are you sure you want to keep me out of trouble?" she asked quietly. She wanted to kiss him really badly. What was the matter with her?

He opened his mouth to answer but a loud, richly dressed young couple came downstairs.

"Are we just going to spend the night on the stairs, or is there actually a bar in this bar?" he asked.

She widened her eyes, and she stopped dead in her tracks. "You know what, I don't even know your name." She tipped her head from one side to the other. "Except, of course, Little Dick." She was hesitating, deliberating. She wanted more time to decide if he was the one. He was an ideal candidate. And her hormones were rioting in her body for release after all the fighting and fear the evening had brought before he'd stepped in to help.

He laughed. "I'm fine if you want to call me that in front of your friends, but the name my mother uses is Dexter, Dex."

"Dexter Dex? That's a strange name," she said.

"Wow. So, so funny. So who are you, Eleanor?"

"Who am I? Do you mean philosophically or are you asking for my name?"

"I'm asking for your name, occupation, you know, easy things like that. The philosophical stuff can come later."

"There's going to be a later?" she asked, taking a deep breath as though that very idea was the most unlikely thing she had heard in her life. Her hormones were telling her otherwise.

He smiled at her, as if he could see what she was contemplating. "Let's have a drink, and discuss," he said.

She nodded and continued up the stairs. Alcohol was what she needed to make sense of the ricocheting feelings inside her.

Was she going to do this? Was she going to release her stress with this British pilot who had a sexy Daniel Craig accent?

She wanted to see his slow blink when she touched him. She wanted to hear him call her name with that accent. She wanted to hear about the infamous Ironman.

"Drinks it is," she said as he brushed shoulders with her.

"As long as I don't end up wearing it, or with a broken nose."

"Well if you manage to not be a dick, then I think you should be fine."

"Eh. No promises. What did that guy say to you to make you punch him like that?" Dex asked.

She hesitated for a moment. She wasn't going to tell him that Munster had questioned her ability. Well not her ability, just her temperament. And that he'd accused her of sleeping her way into her rank. Or that she was a daddy's girl, or any variation of the things she'd heard so many times before. Of course, she realized punching him in the nose probably wasn't the best way to persuade her fellow pilots that she did have the right temperament for the job. But there had been extenuating circumstances. Mr. Hollywood and his goons.

"It's fine if you don't want to tell me," her companion said. "But don't lie to me."

"Why would you think I was going to lie?" she asked, deeply concerned that he could see through her eyes to her soul.

"Those pauses you make when I ask you a simple question.

I know that you're trying to formulate a lie or fudge the answer. You don't need to lie to me. I'm not going to judge you." He paused. "Much."

"So, let's not ask each other any difficult questions, and we won't have to lie to each other."

"I think it's sweet that you think I was going to lie to you," he said.

"You're a man, and your lips move. Of course you'll lie to me."

"Wow. Okay, I think we need a drink and you can tell me all about your deep mistrust of men."

"I mistrust women too," she said with a smile.

Several seconds passed before she realized he had taken her hand again. She didn't know whether to smile or to shake his hand off. As they approached the door at the top of the stairs, it opened.

"Hey, Bees," the bouncer said, leaning forward and offering his cheek to her.

She kissed it and squeezed his huge arm. "Hey, Dickens, how are you?"

"Doing so much better to see you here. It's been too long." He looked Dexter over. "And it's definitely been too long since you brought someone here."

"Dexter, Dickens. Dickens, Dexter," she introduced.

"Good to meet you, Dickens," he said.

"You too. Well done, my man. And good luck," Dickens said, ducking a fake swipe from Eleanor.

"I'm getting the impression I'm going to need it," Dex said, shaking his hand.

"Can we go upstairs?" she asked, shaking her head at the pair of them.

"Of course you can. Go right on up."

They pushed through a curtain into the main bar. A thick bass beat thumped in time to a violet flickering light. She went to the foot of the ornate stairs and one of the younger bouncers unclipped his velvet rope and let them up without a word.

Upstairs it was like a different world, the music softer, slower, and the lights dimmer.

Dexter was still holding her hand, this man who rescued her. Normally Eleanor didn't like anyone touching her. But for some reason, his hand in hers felt normal, natural even. She nodded at the barman, who waved back, and she moved to a booth along the back of the bar.

They slid into the booth and closed the privacy curtains, and then it occurred to her that she was going to explore this privacy with Dexter. The thought both thrilled and scared her.

They sat opposite each other and suddenly had nothing to say. After a couple of seconds of weird silence, he leaned forward. "So, Eleanor, why did he call you Bees?"

"My call sign is Bees Knees. So…Bees."

"You're a pilot. Of course you're a pilot," he said, leaning back in the booth. He averted his eyes and she realized that he was reliving his brag-fest on the bus.

"Don't feel bad. Meeting you on the bus was definitely the highlight of my day." She smiled, covering her lie. Succeeding in her mission had been the highlight, but given how the rest of the day had unfurled, she figured she was allowed the white lie.

There was another silence as he gazed at her, clearly assessing the veracity of her claim. She said nothing.

He said nothing.

Were they in a "who can break first?" contest all of a sudden? She stared back and crossed her arms. This was going to get them nowhere fast, but fuck if she was going to be the first to crack.

He leaned forward suddenly and took the top off an invisible pen and made to write on the table. "So, Eleanor, why do you want this job?"

She clasped her hands together and leaned forward to mirror him. "I just really, like, love to bomb things?" she said in her best California valley accent.

"And what benefits are you expecting?" he said, pretending to take a note on the table.

She held his gaze and bit her lip. She smiled in the silence.

He cleared his throat and pretended to close his notebook. "Very good. When can you start?"

"Immediately." She grinned, enjoying the game.

His gaze rested on her lips, and she knew in that second that he was hers for the taking. She took a breath and leaned forward—just a couple of inches to see what he would do.

He quirked a very sexy half-smile and leaned toward her.

She closed her eyes, and her heart sped up. Eight years. Eight dry years.

The curtains flew open, and the barman brought them drinks they had not ordered.

He placed in the middle of the table one mai tai with an umbrella and a cherry, and one Scotch on the rocks. Dex looked at the drinks with a frown.

"The barman knows what you want to drink before you want to drink it. It's quite a talent of his," she said. She hesitated for a long second, then picked up the Scotch on the rocks and went to drink it.

Dex's face was a picture. Eleanor laughed and put the glass down again. "Don't worry, the mai tai's mine."

"Not that I wouldn't have drunk it," he said, picking up the Scotch. "I'm really not proud when it comes to alcohol." He laughed with her. She liked the sound of his laugh.

Eleanor took a sip from the straw and savored the sweetness on her tongue. She knew she shouldn't be drinking, but she figured if Dex was going to drink, she could have one too. Besides, after her day? It gave her permission to drink. To drink and think nothing about her father or the jerks from TGO.

Dex took a swallow of his Scotch and put the glass down. "Tell me about yourself. I don't mean the things that you might like to lie to me about, but things about you. Things you love, things you can do without…" He shrugged "How sexy my accent is. How quickly you'll ask me to marry you. You know, things like that." He grinned at her, and somehow in the confinement of their booth she felt as if they were a real couple.

"You have an accent? I didn't notice," she said.

"Then maybe you need to come closer." He patted the table, like the same way he'd pat the seat of a chair to encourage a dog to jump up.

"Closer?" she said doubtfully.

"Much closer."

Well, he asked for it. Of course, she could take the civilized route, slide off her bench, open the curtains to the booth, and slide in his side, but where was the fun in that? She took a long sip from her mai tai and pushed the glasses to one side of the table. Then she slipped her feet onto the bench beneath her and put her knee onto the table.

"Really. You're going there? Across the table?" he said.

"You want me to stop?" she asked, freezing in place. Her face was about ten inches from his, she deliberately blinked rapidly, gazing at him from beneath her eyelashes.

"I do not want you to stop. Come over here and put your arse on the table." He said the words deliberately, with a knowing smile.

"You want me to sit…right there, in front of you?" She tipped her head to one side as if considering his request. In reality she was wondering if she could actually physically contort herself enough to do it. She sat on the table like a mermaid and then swung her legs around, trying not to kick him in the face. She figured at this stage that might be a deal breaker. Or maybe not. He'd already taken a beating for her today. She suspected that he may have been the pilot she shot down earlier—just to add insult to injury. She was going to try not to mention that.

She was in position, as requested. Butt on the table, legs on either side of his thighs. He didn't move, but the intensity of his gaze fluttered her in parts that hadn't fluttered for years. She reached for her drink and took a sip from the straw.

She felt his hands on her feet first. Running his fingers over the arch of her foot in her sandals. It should have tickled, but instead it drove heat up her legs and into her body. His hands stroked up her legs, first her calves, then the tops of her thighs. And without hesitation or asking permission, he slipped his hands around to her inner thighs, hovering just short of her panties.

"What do you want, Eleanor? I want to hear you tell me." His fingers stroked the front of her panties, once, twice, so lightly, there was nothing to press herself against, and she wanted to press herself against him so much.

"I want you to make me come," she said in a surprisingly steady voice. Surprising, because all of her insides were melting. Just saying the words turned her on.

His mouth dropped open very slightly, and his eyes darkened. He slipped his fingers beneath her panties and straight into her wetness.

"How long have you been wet?" he asked.

Her breath was already out of her control. "Since you hit that guy for me," she whispered. She closed her eyes as his fingers found her clit. "You do know where it is…," she said before biting her lip to stop a moan.

With one hand, he'd pulled her panties aside and was playing in her wetness with the other. Circling her clit and then sliding fingers into her. She arched and leaned back on her hands.

"You know I can see every part of you. I can see how wet you are. I can feel it on my fingers. I can see your pussy move when I put my fingers in you. I can feel your muscles clasping them. And all I can think is that I want to bury my cock so far inside you that I'll be able to feel your heart beat against it." He pulled his fingers out and slipped them over her clit again, faster, harder, softer, in circles, driving her crazy, until she felt herself falling over the edge of control.

Her stomach muscles tensed as she moaned in response to her orgasm. "Jesus," she gasped. She slid onto his lap and leaned in to kiss him. He tasted of Scotch and sex and heat. His tongue fought with hers for dominance, until she ceded the victory to him. He deserved it. He assaulted her mouth, and she got a sense that sex would be a similar fight. The thought made her hot again.

CHAPTER NINE

"What are you thinking?" he asked, expecting her to say that she'd never done that before, or that she was embarrassed, or those things that women usually say when they show their dirty, wanton side.

"I was thinking that sex with you would be a battle worth fighting." She leaned back and rocked gently against his erection.

Suddenly he didn't know why he'd expected such a commonplace answer from such an unusual woman. "Do you now?" He looked her in the eye and gently scraped a fingertip over one of her nipples through her dress. "Who do you think would win?"

She arched her back languidly, like a cat. "It depends what the benefits of surrender would be." She tipped her head to the side. "Don't you think?"

"Didn't you just surrender to me?" he asked, holding her

hips still, because God help him, he didn't want to come in his pants. And he was close.

She frowned at him. "And here I was thinking that you'd surrendered to me."

"I'll never surrender to a foreign national," he said, grabbing his drink again to distract him from the woman sitting on top of him. "Queen and country, you know."

"Neither will I," she replied, back stiff with resolve. "Especially not the British. We've already beat you once. Don't make me do it again."

"Well, then, I see an impasse. And by the way, we totally let you win that one. You know what we call Independence Day in the UK? Thanksgiving."

"Those are fighting words." She tried to reach for her mai tai but realized he was holding both her wrists down. She frowned. "Are you scared of a girl?"

"Too right I am. I saw you break that one bloke's nose, and then I saw you punch another one. I have work tomorrow, and I don't want to be too incapacitated." He released her, and she lifted up his hand.

"We forgot the ice," she said, and he got the impression that she was changing the subject.

"I guess it's time we had the talk," he said.

"The talk? The 'it's not you, it's me' talk, or the 'how about a beach wedding' talk?"

"Neither?" He pulled a "calm down with the crazy" expression and she winked at him. "Although, let's go back to the beach wedding discussion later. I meant the talk about who those men were, and why they were after you. I mean, you know it's serious, don't you? Men trying to kidnap a U.S. Air Force pilot? We should have called the police. Homeland Security would definitely need to be involved, I'd have thought. And the fact that you didn't call anyone suggests there's more to this than you're telling me."

She slid off his lap and sat beside him, drink in hand. "It's not as easy as that. I would call the MPs, but it seems Nellis's security forces are all TechGen-One right now—at least for the duration of Red Flag. I would call my father, but I suspect he's with TechGen-One right now—or at least the CEO." She'd said way too much. What she really needed to do was go back to her lodging and call her father in the morning, when she could be reasonably sure he'd be alone.

"What does your father have to do with this?" he asked with a frown.

"My father is General Daniels from this morning's briefing."

"The sound bite bloke is your dad?" he asked with a level of incredulity that Eleanor found quite endearing.

She raised her glass in acknowledgment.

"Okay, but what does he have to do with the type of thugs who can't keep their wrists firm while punching?"

She'd forgotten that he'd taken one for her. "Oh my God, your jaw. How is it?" She ran her fingers lightly over his stubble.

"As I said, he bent his wrist, so the punch was barely anything. But thanks for remembering that I took a punch for you and knocked someone out for you. Does this happen often? Do I need to start taking a tally of what you owe me?"

"How do you think I should pay you back?" she asked with a grin.

He raised an eyebrow. "Let me think on that. Now, back to your father."

She blew air from her cheeks. "I don't know. I think TechGen-One is up to something, or at least someone at the company is. I don't know what it is. I just know that they see me as a threat. I overheard part of a conversation my father had with the CEO—Danvers—and they didn't seem to like that." She didn't want to give any more detail about her father, because she didn't know how involved he was—if he was.

She looked away. Of course he was involved. She'd clearly heard that whatever was going down was worth billions, and it had sounded like her own father had given her up to the men who had tried to persuade her not to talk. She bit her lip. She wondered why her instinct was to protect him when he was clearly not going to protect her.

And then there was another problem: How could she get back on base without them noticing? The only way would be to blend in with the people leaving the mixer in the buses. If she called a taxi, they'd run her ID as soon as she got to base, just like they did for any car entering. On a bus, they generally just swiped the driver's ID and then just got everyone else to hold theirs up.

Shit. Was she being paranoid? She had no frame of reference for what was happening to her. She just needed to speak to her father and get him to tell her what the hell she'd gotten involved in.

"I've got to go," she said. "I've got to get back to the Paris casino to ride the bus to base. What's the time? Do you think they're still there?"

"Well, now I just feel used," he said with a deadpan expression.

She hesitated. "I didn't mean…"

"Gotcha." He looked at his watch. "It's one p.m. No, wait, that's not right. It's nine p.m." He shrugged. "Time zone problems. I think on our in-brief paperwork it said that the last bus would leave at nine thirty to ensure everyone was back on base safely."

"Have you done the mixer before? Do they check everyone's IDs, or just wave them through on to base?" she asked, fumbling for her purse and straightening her hair.

"I can't remember. It was three years ago when I was last here. Come on, let's make like shepherds." He got out of the booth and held his hand out to her.

She took it with a questioning look. "Make like shepherds?"

He threw thirty bucks on the table for the drinks. "Get the flock out of here."

She insisted that he not be seen with her, in case the people after her made him a target, too, even though Dex figured his altercation with that guy may have already painted him with whatever brush Eleanor had been painted with. His whole world had been turned around and twisted inside out over the past four hours.

He followed her to the bus, keeping his eyes open for

anyone who might have been looking for her. Was TechGen-One—the company everyone raved about—really after her for some overheard conversation? It sounded crazy to him. Like he'd stepped into a scene out of a movie. He just didn't know what part he was supposed to play. He sighed. He could also be getting *Punk'd*. There was always that.

They got back to the Paris in good time. The bus was just pulling up into the hotel forecourt. Unfortunately, the bloke Eleanor had hit at the mixer was also there.

"No. You are not getting on this bus with me. You're dangerous," he shouted as Eleanor walked up to the bus.

She ignored him, didn't even look at him. Dex admired her restraint but figured it probably had something to do with the possibility of getting disciplined for it the following day. What had she gotten herself into, and why did he feel invested in it?

He stood at the back of the line and rolled his neck. She was surprising. Gorgeous, sexy as all hell, but he had to remember he was here for a reason. He had to leave Red Flag on top of his game.

He saw a scuffle and stepped out of line to make sure it wasn't her. It was. Without thinking, he raced to the top of the queue. Eleanor was pulling her arm away from the guy with the broken nose, and two other people were pulling him away from her. Just as he was about to stand down, the guy tore himself free from the people holding him and launched himself at Dex.

Dex easily sidestepped his attempt to rush him, and the man fell to the pavement. He just sat there, head bowed in defeat. Dex felt bad for him and offered him his hand. The dude took it and pulled himself up, but as soon as he was on his feet, he swung again. Dex could feel the fist coming toward him before he even saw it. He bent his body away from the blow and had to hold the guy up so he didn't fall over when his swing hit only air. He was drunk. Really, really drunk.

The worst thing was that Dex's first thought wasn't for Eleanor's safety; it was thinking that at least one pilot from the American team would be too drunk to fly tomorrow. If his team had any luck, this tosser here would be in the Aggressor Squadron, and they'd be flying one down tomorrow. Then he thought about Eleanor. Was she in the Aggressor Squadron?

Fuck, this was not why he'd come to Vegas—to get involved in someone else's shit, no matter how attractive that someone was. He wasn't interested in her, or her father, or TechGen-One, or—he looked at the guy he was holding up—him, or anything. He knew he shouldn't have come to the fucking mixer. Next time someone else was taking one for the team.

He leaned the drunk man against the bus stop and walked away, refusing to meet Eleanor's eyes. He was a fucking bastard for it, but he had to keep his head in his game. Not just for him, but for the rest of his team and the RAF.

CHAPTER TEN

Eleanor watched Dex leave. He must have heard Munster talk about sleeping her way to her rank.

Goddamn that bastard. He knew just what buttons to press to make her mad. And she'd let him. Again, he'd suggested in front of everyone that she wasn't fit for command. That it really had been her father, and nameless, imagined men who pulled the strings to put her in the running as Killer's replacement next year. She wondered if he would report her for the altercation at the mixer. It was a toss-up—would he want to get her in trouble or would he want to protect his reputation? Being beaten up by a girl did not look good for a hotshot pilot. But he'd also want the promotion that she'd got over him. Damn him.

She took a breath. What had she done to her career? And did it even matter if TGO heavies were shoving her in front of moving limos?

She avoided everyone's eyes and waited to climb onto the

bus. Truth was, no one in the squadron took her seriously, even though she'd been the best pilot for two years. Every time she was more accurate, faster, more cunning, and beat them in an exercise, they claimed their aircraft wasn't working properly or something else had "let" her win. She really wasn't sure why she bothered.

And now she'd given them a double whammy. She'd given him an excuse to report her, and she'd be up all night worrying about the consequences. No way she'd be performing at her peak tomorrow.

Exasperated at herself, she kicked the tire of a van that was at the curb. The window rolled down to reveal one of the base airmen who acted as designated drivers for troops who had one too many. She squeezed her eyes closed. Another witness to her crazy.

"Ma'am? Can I drive you back to base?" the young man asked, politely not mentioning her kicking at his vehicle.

She was done. If the TGO fuckers wanted to haul her in as she went through security, she was inclined to let them. She no longer had the energy to fight. She took a deep breath and smiled. "Yes, you can. Thank you."

As soon as the word *yes* left her lips, he jumped out and opened the door for her. She purposefully didn't look for Dex or anyone else. She wanted the van to herself.

The airman was very tall and fit, which was probably why he'd been chosen to pick up partiers in Vegas. As she got in, he did a double take. "Ma'am!" he said urgently. "Are you hurt? You have blood on your dress. Are you hurt?" he repeated. Fear and professionalism battled across his face.

She held up her hand to stop the racing of his thoughts. "I'm fine." She looked down at the smear of blood on her shoulder and smiled. "You should see the other guy."

"Are you f—" He corrected himself. "…kidding me? Who tried to hurt you, ma'am? Just point him out to me." He stood at attention—whether he realized it or not—and looked ready to jump into the fray on her behalf.

She took a second and stopped thinking about herself and her own pity party. This man, who only knew her by her rank, was ready to protect and defend her, as she would him in the same situation. This was why she worked so damn hard to be the best pilot possible. Not for trophies, but to protect the troops on the ground—the ones who relied on her for cover, to neutralize the enemy.

Tension seeped out of her shoulders and she felt them drop a good couple of inches. She smiled. "I really appreciate you having my back. But everything's okay now. I just need my cot."

He looked into her eyes, trying to see if she was being forthcoming. But he'd been given an order, and with one more careful look at the people outside the casino, he nodded. "Of course, ma'am."

She slumped in the back and tried not to catch his eye as he got in and they pulled away.

Back at the base, a woman gave her only a cursory look while scanning her ID. No sirens. No alarms. No heavily muscled men emerging to drag her away. Relieved, she strode back to her lodging, threw her dress into the laundry, and got into bed. It was way too late to have regrets, and she absolved herself of her guilt, if only for the night so she could sleep. She'd get up early and deal with everything then. Fucking Dale Munster. TGO. Her father. She just hoped she still had a job in the morning.

As she went to sleep, she thought about Dexter. Wondering if she'd see him again. If he'd even want to see her again. Munster's words reverberated in her head. If Dexter had heard them, she'd never see him again.

CHAPTER ELEVEN

D_{ex} had his mind in the game. He absolutely, positively wasn't thinking about Eleanor's face as she came or the sharp repartee they'd shared. Or how her dress had hitched up under her when she'd crawled across the table. Nope, nothing to see here.

He was definitely not wondering if she'd spoken to her father, got the TechGen-One thing sorted out, or what she looked like when she'd just woken up. His brain was abso-fucking-lutely 100 percent focused on the day's mission.

Why hadn't he said anything to her in the bus line? Why hadn't he got her number? Why hadn't he asked to see her again?

Because he needed to concentrate. *And how's that working out for you, you dumb-arse?*

How could it work out when all he could think about was tasting her?

"Sir?" A voice penetrated his daydream.

"Yes?" He turned to see Matthews holding out his hand for the spanner Dex was holding. Fuck.

"Sorry, I was…thinking about the mission." He handed the wrench over and took himself outside the hangar so he wouldn't have to talk to any—

"Top o' the morning to you, Flight Lieutenant."

Dexter groaned as he recognized the voice. The Animal, of course. "You know that's Irish, right? I'm English. A good old, plain 'good morning' would be fine," he said.

"But where's the fun in that?" the Animal replied, throwing a cigarette directly into his mouth. He never smoked them; he just liked tossing them into his mouth. It did round out his image of the coolest bloke on base, Dex conceded.

They shook hands, and just as Dex was about to ask the Animal whether he'd survived the previous day's mission, a loud voice made him jump.

"Animaaaal," a woman yelled almost next to his ear.

"Darling! They still letting you fly with the big boys?" The Animal held out his arms, and Dex turned.

A woman in a flight suit and a blue U.S. Air Force hat jumped into his arms. They squeezed each other for a second, and then she dropped her feet back to the ground. "You've been in the showers with the guys in my squadron." She dropped her voice to a whisper. "You know they're not big boys."

The Animal cackled. "So true, so true."

She looked at Dex, her hand already outstretched as if to shake. He automatically extended his right hand. And then he realized who it was, at the same time she recognized him.

Her jaw dropped.

He couldn't think of anything to say—especially in front of the Animal. The silence between them extended uncomfortably.

"Well, this isn't awkward at all," she said.

"Eleanor," Dex said, his voice suddenly gravelly.

The Animal looked at Dex, then at Eleanor, and then back at Dex. He slapped his hands on both his knees and howled. Literally, like a fucking wolf. "You two? This is going to be so much fun."

Frankly the most cringe-inducing thing about the situation was just how embarrassed Eleanor looked to see him. Her head was down, and she looked like a high school cheerleader trying to avoid the nerd who was following her around. It kind of pissed him off.

"Clearly *fun* is not the right word," Dex said, putting his aviators on.

She said nothing for a second, making the Animal look at them both as if he were watching a tennis match. Her silence made him wonder if he'd misread her awkwardness.

"Wow. I'm sorry I'm no fun," she said, her voice cold as ice.

Everything inside him wanted to reassure her, but with the Animal lapping up every word, he hesitated. His lack of response hung in the air.

"Wow," she repeated, looking away.

"Oh, come on," Dex said, trying to ease the tension between them. "The only fun we really have is up there." He nodded toward the sky. "It's all that matters, isn't it?" He was appealing to her love of flying, but as the words left his mouth, he realized that it sounded like he was dismissing their evening together.

Her mouth dropped open again, and the Animal looked askance at him. And if even the Animal realized Dex had put his foot in his mouth, then he really had. He opened his mouth to apologize, but she cut him off.

"Well, let's not take that risk again." She shoved on her aviators. "Let's go have some real fun."

"Great idea," he said automatically. *Jesus. What the fuck is wrong with me?*

She raised her eyebrows. "I'm going to be looking for you up there. I mean, it's only fun, right?" She looked over his shoulder and found somebody else to talk to. "Missy! Come rescue me from these useless men."

The Animal protested. "Hey, don't lump me in with him." He pointed at Dex, but Eleanor had already left. "Ironman, you need to learn how to speak to women. I thought you Brits were full of good manners and tea and politeness. Maybe a little cricket."

"Yeah, I must be running on empty." He really did need to get breakfast. He was just going to put it down to hunger. Except he knew very well that it wasn't, that she had crawled under his skin and taken up residence there. Like a scarab beetle. "I'll apologize later." Again.

"The club. Don't forget. Tonight," the Animal said as he walked away, not giving Dex an opportunity to refuse the invitation.

CHAPTER TWELVE

As Dex sat in his aircraft awaiting takeoff, he took a deep breath. He pulled his shoulders right up to his ears and then allowed them to drop, urging the tension from them. It usually worked. It didn't today.

The Blue Team had collaborated on a new strategy. Their official, sanctioned goal was to destroy a munitions plant close to the base.

He had guessed that the Aggressor Squadron would assume they would head straight for the plant, try to get there faster than them, and lie in wait, picking them off as they arrived. That was not going to happen.

As soon as they had all taken off, they disappeared—out of formation, each taking a quadrant on the farther side of the target. They would be coming from the opposite direction. And they weren't going in to drop bombs—their objective was to neutralize the Aggressors first, to go at them hard and fast, while they waited for them from the south.

They pushed up high, higher than a bombing mission would dictate, and thrust into supersonic, circumventing the range the munition plant was on.

"Blue Sniper One, approaching outer quadrant. Slowing to subsonic," he said to his wingmen.

"Blue Four, already here. Patrolling the outer eastern marker," Ginger said.

"Blue Three, ditto, on the western edge," Heinrich, from the German Luftwaffe said.

"Blue Two. Due north of the range."

Everyone was in place. "On my mark, turn into formation and drop to one thousand feet."

Three clicks came back.

Dex watched the desert fly beneath him. "Three, two, one. Execute," he said.

Less than two minutes later, they were in formation, approaching the patrolling Aggressors from the northwest, instead of the south.

"Oh my God. Look. I think this is going to work," Ginger said.

The Aggressors were flying in formation, south of the target. For a second he wondered if they could get straight in and do a bombing run before their opponents even realized the Blue Team was there. "Blue Two and Blue Three—take that target out. We'll cover you."

"Copy that."

"Ginger—let's scatter them. Take out the trailer." There

was one aircraft flying to the rear—always the most vulnerable. He could feel the victory pumping his blood.

Glory was theirs. All they had to do was take it.

The Aggressors had been patrolling the site for thirty minutes. "Something isn't right," Eleanor murmured.

She looked over at Killer. Like all of them, his head seemed as if it were on a swivel. They checked the horizon toward the airfield but saw nothing. "Maybe something happened on the ground," Munster commented.

Eleanor rolled her eyes but said nothing. Their ground control would have given them a heads-up if there was an operational problem. She figured discretion would be a good thing today. She'd tried not to catch Munster's eye in the briefing, and he hadn't said a word to her, so she suspected that someone had talked him off the ledge. Not that she necessarily deserved the break.

Something felt a little off with her controls. It was weird. The aircraft was fine, but it just felt like there was chewing gum around the base of the joystick—it seemed a little sluggish. Could Munster have sabotaged…no. No way. None of them would risk someone else's life. She shook it off, since their crew chief had assured her that they'd been through all the planes from nose to tail, ensuring they were in flight condition.

"Red Viper Four, you're dead. Back to base," their controller said.

"What the…?" Killer said, over the sound of Munster cursing his luck.

The four remaining aircraft scattered. Eleanor broke hard to the left, attaining an altitude that would allow her to see where the Blue Team was. She virtually inverted her aircraft to get a good look.

Pulling around, she saw the shadow of a Typhoon against the gray of the rock below them. Dammit, he was above her. She spun down and away over a ridge to see if she could come back into the target area without a tail. Her bandit was right on her. He wasn't going to let her regroup.

"Red Viper Two—you're also dead. Come on home," the controller said.

And then there were three. Flares popped out of nowhere, and she dived away to avoid them, then brought her Viper up as fast as she could. Her vertical ascent swept by the Typhoon too fast to see who was in it. But there was no voice telling her to go home, so that was something.

And then seven aircraft appeared on her radar. What the fuck? "Killer—I'm seeing seven bandits on my radar."

"I've got nothing on mine. But I do have one on my tail. I'd appreciate an assist." He groaned as he pulled a tight maneuver. "He's right on me."

"And I'm right on him," she said, firing her flares. She was right on target. The Typhoon bugged out as she watched.

"Good kill," said the controller on the ground.

"I've got seven…" Her radar was now clear. "Scratch that." That was weird. Maybe it was another sortie she'd caught. Her radar fritzed and then came back online. Her eyes were glued to it—she'd never seen any kind of static on it before.

A Typhoon bum-rushed her airspace, so close that she instinctively pulled up and away to the left to avoid a collision. Bastard. She pushed on the throttle and sped after him. She inched closer, waiting for her targeting system to tell her she was in range, when her radio crackled.

"Red Viper Three—you're dead. Blue Team's bombing mission was successful. All players back on deck." Fuck. Killer was their only survivor. "Sorry, Killer," she said.

"Just another day of infamy," he replied drily.

It was a rookie mistake, chasing a distraction—in this case, an aircraft fleeing the scene and easy to catch up with—and then taking incoming fire from behind. If only her radar hadn't freaked the fuck out, she wouldn't have been distracted by that either. But there was no way she was going to say that when she landed. She wasn't going to be that kind of pilot. She'd have a quiet word with the chief later in the day.

The weight of failure felt as heavy as g-force. When was the last time she'd failed a mission? When was the last time another pilot had gotten the better of her?

So far Red Flag was not turning out the way she'd expected. Not by a long shot.

CHAPTER THIRTEEN

After a celebration and short debrief with his team, Dex hit the showers, got dressed, and headed to the officers' club on Nellis.

He didn't want to go, although to be fair, drinking as a victor was sure better than drinking as a loser. It had been such an easy bait-and-switch strategy—one that would keep the Aggressor Squadron up that night he was sure.

With a resounding victory under his belt, he was more concerned with apologizing to Eleanor for the comment he'd made that morning. He hoped he could mai tai some forgiveness from her.

But right now, he needed a Scotch. And he needed to get this initiation thing over and done with—whatever the Animal had been talking about earlier. In truth, he didn't want to have any part in what the Animal had in store for him, but he knew if he didn't, he would get more hassle for not going than he would for showing up. Some things were best to just suck up.

The bar area was fairly full. Ginger and Tinker, their other Typhoon pilot, were already there, and he nodded at them, twirling his finger in the air to ask if they needed another round. They gave him the thumbs-up. Of course they did.

He ordered a Scotch and soda for himself and a couple of pints for the other guys, then took the drinks back to the table.

"What a fucking bees' bollocks of a day," Tinker said, raising his glass.

They all raised their glasses before taking the first sip. "No kidding," Dex said. Nevertheless, the Scotch tasted wrong, and everything felt wrong. He looked for her. He wanted to make it right. He suddenly wondered if anything would feel right if he didn't speak to her.

"We better come up with a great counter-strategy for tomorrow too. We've got the lay of the land, we know what sneaky bastards the Aggressors are, and we'll be ready for them again," Dexter said, leaning back in the booth.

"I'll drink to that," Ginger said, downing half his pint in practically one gulp.

Thankfully, the following day's mission didn't start with the briefing until 2:00 p.m. That meant they could drink until midnight and be good to fly. He knew none of them would, even though Ginger was beginning to look as if he could sink twelve pints in the next hour, because they all knew better. A few drinks, a meal, early to bed, and then up for breakfast and PT. Plenty of time for all alcohol to leave the system.

"Uh-oh," Tinker said. "Prepare for the storm."

"Ironmaaan!" the Animal shouted from the bar. Everyone quieted down—as they always did—to see what the Animal was going to do or say next.

Better get it over and done with, Dex thought. He had other things to concentrate on. Like Eleanor.

Nope. Like winning. Maybe winning and Eleanor. Maybe winning Eleanor...

"Everyone, everyone. Listen up—I have an announcement to make," the Animal said.

Dex cracked his neck to one side, trying to relieve some of the tension. He finished his Scotch in one gulp and placed the glass back on the table.

"Gather round, gather round," the Animal said, dragging a chair over to their booth and sitting astride it.

Pretty much everyone in the bar gravitated to their booth. But as soon as everyone piled around, Dex could suddenly see Eleanor. She stayed at the bar, her back to him. Clearly she wasn't going to make it easy for him to apologize, and rightly so. At least she was here and not in some base jail somewhere.

"As many of you know," the Animal said, "our friend and fellow warrior Ironman choked on the dust last year, flying a sortie in Afghanistan. While he undoubtedly bit the big one, he managed to steer his aircraft away from a field clinic, smash it into the ground"—he mimed a huge explosion with his hands—"and walk away with only a couple of broken bones." The Animal deliberately nodded in approval at the crowd as they erupted in applause.

Dex hung his head and closed his eyes. Jesus. People were applauding him for crashing his aircraft. He couldn't believe that this was his life now. From ace to pity party in one short year.

"There are not many of us here who would get back in the saddle after getting dirt poisoning. But this man did. And so he joins an illustrious club, short on members but long on war stories. I am today inducting Flight Lieutenant Dexter "Ironman" Stone into the annals of the Saddle Club." He stopped for more raucous shouting and applause.

If Dex could have sunk into the floor and escaped through a trapdoor, he would.

"Fellow members come forward." The Animal rose from his chair, rolled up his left uniform sleeve, and along with three other pilots—all with rolled up sleeves—showed the unofficial Saddle Club patch sewn onto the inside of his sleeve.

Dex stood up and did his duty. He smiled, nodded, and shook the hands of his fellow club members. When the Animal shook his hand, he transferred the patch seamlessly to Dexter's hand, as if he were coining him.

"Thanks, guys. And a special thank you for reminding me of the one day in my life I've spent the last year trying to forget."

Everyone cheered and raised their glasses at him. He raised his empty one back.

"Thank you for celebrating the fact that I crashed my aircraft, costing the good British taxpayer a mere forty million pounds. If anyone would like to pass the hat around so I can buy a new one, please feel free."

Everyone laughed, and as the crowd dispersed, pilots he didn't even know lined up to shake his hand.

As terrible as it was to his ego, he felt good knowing that if he was in combat again, he would be flying with these allied pilots. "Seriously?" he called out to the dispersing audience. "Is nobody going to buy me a drink? No?"

A couple people laughed but walked away. Dex sat down and looked to his empty glass. Out of the corner of his eye, he saw Tinker and Ginger jump to their feet, and he did the same, assuming a higher-ranking officer was present.

There wasn't. Eleanor was standing there with a Scotch in one hand and what looked like a mai tai in the other. Just the visual brought back visceral memories from the night before. His dick tightened.

Dexter hesitated, and in that second Tinker and Ginger totally abandoned him and made haste to the bar. "Great wingmen you are," he called at their backs.

He looked at Eleanor. "Let me guess, the cocktail is for me." He sat down and motioned for her to take Tinker's empty seat. He watched as she hesitated but felt a small thrill when she sat down.

"At least you didn't crash today," she said, passing him the Scotch.

He blew out a breath and smiled. "Yup. Today we bathed in the sweet scented oils of victory. How did you do?"

"Tomorrow will be a better day." She took a sip of her cocktail.

"It was that bad?" he asked.

She put her drink down and looked up. "You were flying a Typhoon today?"

"Yeee…" He dragged the word out. "No. Yes. Maybe. Why?"

She gave a mirthless laugh. "Fair enough." He took a sip and looked at her, marveling at how different she looked every time he saw her. Last night in a sundress, this morning in a flight suit with no makeup, and this evening with her hair down and wearing a denim skirt and a plain gray T-shirt. It was as if she were three different people—a party girl, a professional pilot, and the girl next door.

"When do you fly tomorrow?" she asked.

"In the afternoon. It's a long-range mission, apparently. I think we get our briefing around two p.m., and as far as I can tell, we're not due back until after nightfall. What about you?"

"I'm waiting for a text. My squadron is the biggest, so I'm assuming I won't fly every day." She didn't seem to mind, but Dex couldn't imagine being here and not flying. Anytime he wasn't actually flying, he had to distract himself by any means possible to take his mind off the fact that his whole body, and every cell in it, wanted to be in the air.

He took his opportunity. "I'm sorry about this morning," he said. "I'm not usually that ungracious."

"So, who are you really? The white knight who came to my rescue last night, the rogue who made me come on a bar table, or the man who insulted me this morning?" she asked over the rim of her drink.

"I would say I vector somewhere between those three. A white knight rogue who only opens his mouth to change feet." He had to try and dig himself out of this one. "Which one would you prefer I be this evening?" he asked, knowing that her answer would infer that they would in fact be spending the evening together.

"I haven't decided yet," she said. She bit her lip and stared at him for an uncomfortable couple of seconds. "Maybe there's another Ironman I haven't seen yet?"

"There are many. So, no arrests? Did you get to see your father?" he asked, the exploits of the previous night returning like a bout of food poisoning. Why had he brought that up?

"My father wouldn't see me this morning, but told me to 'behave.'" She used her fingers to punctuate the quote.

"So, you think that's it on the TGO thing?" he asked, happy that the movie he'd seemed to have stepped into last night wasn't a horror flick.

"I just don't know. It doesn't feel like it." Her mind seemed to be somewhere else. "Do you want to get out of here?" she asked abruptly.

"You asking me out on a date?" he countered with a smile.

She grinned. "Maybe slightly. I mean barely, really."

"Will you be…getting bare?" he asked.

"Pffft. After the way you spoke to me this morning…"

He still hadn't apologized for that. "I'm really sorry about that. I just…"

"Couldn't help yourself?"

"I don't know what got into me. I couldn't stop my mouth from moving and all these alien words from coming out." He pulled a "forgive me" face and she rolled her eyes.

She looked at her unfinished mai tai. "Let's just take a drive. Grab something to eat," she said, getting up and leaving him no option but to get up too.

"Why don't you let me take you to dinner?" he asked.

"I have a better idea," she said.

His dick twitched in his pants. He should definitely stay away from her, but not one part of his body agreed with his brain.

"I'm in your hands."

"What are you waiting for then? Come on."

He started to the door so he could hold it open for her.

"Hey, don't forget your loser patch," she said, and even without looking he knew she had a shit-eating grin on her face.

He turned and grabbed it. "Thanks for the reminder." He shoved it in his pocket. Why did these guys think that a reminder of an epic failure was cool? But he knew he'd have to do it. As long as he survived Red Flag, that was.

He followed her out of the bar, not really caring who watched and what they may think. That was the nice thing about Red Flag, since nobody was going to see each other again, nobody really cared what anyone got up to off the clock. Except for the brass, that was.

She got into a dark blue Audi convertible. They must pay American pilots better than they pay British ones. "Nice car," he said.

"It's a rental. It's fast and comfortable, and that's all I really care about."

"You must care about something else; otherwise you would have got a Ford Focus."

She laughed. "You've got a point there. I like the way it feels when I'm driving it. I like its responsiveness and its smoothness whether I'm going fast or slow. Kind of like my aircraft." She pressed a button and the roof pulled down.

He grabbed his sunglasses from his pocket and put them on. She took hers from on top of the sun visor. "What do you do when you're not flying?"

"Think about flying," she said with a smile. "You?"

He laughed. "About the same."

"Is that why you got back in the saddle?" she asked.

"Yeah. I've been flying since I was seventeen. It's who I am. The thought of not flying was worse than the fear of crashing." What was he saying? Was that true? He had definitely never said that out loud. But maybe that's because nobody had asked him before. He never really socialized with pilots anymore. He spent more time working, more time concentrating, more time wondering what he could have done differently in that last flight in Afghanistan.

"It's something I've never thought about, never wanted to think about," she said. "But I guess no pilot thinks they're going to crash or have to bail out."

"Really? You've never thought about that? Even when you're in the simulator? You've never wondered what would happen if a bird hit your engine or you stalled coming out of supersonic?" He'd always considered that, even before he crashed.

"No. I know what I would do. I practiced it a million times in the simulator. I don't need to think about it, so I don't." She used her turn signal and pulled onto a dirt road.

Dex envied her complete confidence. He guessed that was what he was like before the crash. He wanted to ask where they were going, but in truth as long as they were going together, who cared?

About ten minutes up the highway to the north, she pulled over behind a trailer on the side of the road. A food truck.

"You trust me?" she asked, getting out of the car.

"Not even slightly," he said.

"Not even to order for you?" she asked.

He hesitated for effect, then grinned. "Sure. Go for your life."

She shook her head and disappeared around the front of the truck. Within minutes she was back with a full paper bag. She handed it to him, and he stuck it between his feet.

"You're going to thank me after this meal," she said with a grin.

The smell was enough to make his stomach rumble. "Where will we be eating?"

"You'll see," she replied. "We're nearly there." She turned onto a small road, no more than a path, really.

As they drove down the dirt road, the rocky landscape seemed to glow red in the sunset. He remembered flying over the Grand Canyon in a commercial jet one time and wondering at the color of the rock. In England all the rock was slate gray; in America there were so many different colors. She pulled the car over at the base of a rocky incline and jumped out.

"Come with me," she said. Without looking at him, she reached behind her and held out her hand. He smiled. This was becoming a habit. A habit he didn't mind at all.

He took her hand and allowed her to take the lead. Not that he knew where he was going. After a few minutes, she drew him up next to her. "There," she said.

He looked out at the view. It was the whole of Las Vegas, tiny flickering lights coming on against the falling dusk. The setting sun reflected the deep red rock in Eleanor's sunglasses.

"Sometimes I think this is the only place where Las Vegas looks beautiful," she said. "Look." She pointed.

They both stood there and watched their Red Flag colleagues take off from the runway at Nellis. Tiny specks in the distance, ascending five thousand feet one after the other. "Night missions. I'm glad mine isn't on until tomorrow."

"I'm glad too," she said. She turned to look at him and he realized she was still wearing her sunglasses. And he was still holding her hand.

Gently, he removed her sunglasses and trailed them slowly across her T-shirt. Her lower lip dropped a fraction of an inch as the sunglasses scraped her nipple through the material.

Oh yeah, he wanted her. His whole body ignited just at

the move of her lower lip. He slipped his hand around the back of her neck and drew her to him.

Eleanor could barely believe this was happening. She was actually kissing him. Kissing him like he was the last man on earth. Dex was not like anyone she'd met before. Not like any other guy she'd wanted before. The other pilots in her squadron were either dicks like Munster, married, or gay. Or women, and although she had been picked up by a woman before, mostly she wanted the arrogance and hardness of a man's body.

He pulled her roughly to him, holding her hard against him. His lips were firm against hers, and like last night he didn't hesitate to take what he wanted. She wondered how much he wanted and what it would be like. She didn't want to waste time, making him question whether she wanted him or not.

If she wasn't going to reign victorious at Red Flag, she was going to reign victorious right here, right now.

He pulled away from her for a second. "I know this feels amazing right now." He stroked his hand from her hair, down to her peaked nipple, and past it to her waist. "But we have to be clear about what's happening here. I need to know—"

She interrupted him. "I know what's happening here. I'm not a child. This is now, and right here. Not there." She pointed at the air force base, where aircraft were still taking off. "And not here, either." She tapped her finger against his forehead. "I live here, and you live a million miles from here."

"Not exactly a million…," he said. "But getting back to the subject at hand, I was going to ask if you had a handy condom or…"

"I have long-term contraception, and I've been celibate for…a while."

"A while as in weeks or in decades?" He grinned.

"Are you asking if I'm rusty? If I need…flight supervision?" She pulled off her T-shirt in a fast move. "Do I seem like I need a manual?"

He opened his mouth to speak, but his eyes were on her breasts. "No," he said in a hoarse voice. He pulled the zipper on her skirt and with a small wriggle, it fell to the rocky ground. He grinned at her half-outraged, half-turned-on expression.

"Wow," she said under her breath.

"Take off your underwear," he demanded, folding his arms across his chest. He sat on a rock, not taking his eyes off her. "Come on, love. We don't have all day."

So, it was like that, was it? Maybe he expected her to balk at the request. But she didn't. Not for a second. She didn't work out every day to be embarrassed about being naked. She slowly undid her bra, holding it in position with her arm, and slipped the straps down her arms.

His eyes darkened as he watched. He sat, not taking his eyes off her. "Jesus," he said under his breath as she dropped the bra.

She started to kick off her cowboy boots so she could take her panties off, but he stopped her with a hand.

"Nope. You can leave those on." He grinned. "Bloody hell. This must be my lucky day."

She wobbled on her feet—so excited at standing virtually naked, which somehow felt more daring than being totally naked, and watching his dick strain against his pants as he watched her. Heat rose in her body.

"Come here," he said, holding out a hand.

She moved closer. He roughly pulled her against him and his open mouth. Heat flooded through her as his hot breath permeated her panties. Both his hands held her to his mouth, his fingers digging into her ass.

His tongue pressed against her, grinding against her clitoris. Damn her panties. She wanted to be closer, feel closer, wanted him inside her. Inside her head, her heart, her body.

Teeth scraped down her, playing with the hot line between pain and pleasure. He pushed her panties to one side and pulled her into his mouth, until he was sucking on her clit. Her knees felt like honey inside, hot and unsteady. "I've been dreaming about this since you showed me your pussy last night," he said, his voice rumbling against her.

He lifted one of her legs and put it on the rock he was sitting on, allowing him more access, deeper access. She jumped and moaned as she felt her entire body arch to absorb the touch of his tongue. He ran his tongue over her as he slid fingers inside her. His tongue floated against her clitoris, leaving her almost straining into her orgasm. She arched her back and looked up toward the skies. Her home. She was between two homes, the one up there and the place Dex was taking her to right then. Fireworks erupted inside her as she spasmed around his fingers and against his mouth.

"I need you. I need to be in you," he breathed against her.

She agreed. She'd never wanted anyone like this before. Like she'd explode if she didn't totally own him. She stood, holding on to his shoulder as a wave of light-headedness came over her.

He didn't wait. He yanked his jeans off and in one motion swept his T-shirt over his head.

She stood back and slipped off her panties over her boots. Suddenly she felt a little stupid still in her footwear, but his gaze and expression told her not to be. "You're beautiful. Fast and responsive, like your Viper," he whispered.

"So are you," she said, taking in his hard, smooth, muscled body and hard dick.

"What do you want me to do?" he asked.

"If I'm like my aircraft, why don't you take me out for a spin?" she said, tipping her head to one side.

"Your wish…" He picked her up and stood her facing the smooth, red rock. He firmly but slowly stroked her from her neck down her back, dipping between her legs and stroking her once more. She whimpered. He nudged her legs open and slid his dick between them. He was hard and stiff, and she wanted to feel more of him. She bent farther and spread her legs for him.

He groaned and plunged into her, making her cry out with pleasure. Her heart raced, her nipples scraped against the rock, a glorious friction that intensified as he plowed into her.

He pulled her upright, an arm around her waist, and fucked her, filling her up. He dipped his fingers to her clit again and stroked her in time to his thrusts. She clenched around him as she came, hard and fast. He let go and, groaning, came inside her.

She stretched against him, raising her arms and feeling every muscle relax. He cupped her breasts as she did.

He pulled her around and kissed her, gently at first, and then with more insistence. He broke away. "Jesus. There is nothing about you I don't want. Your smell, your taste, your smart mouth, your pussy, your kisses."

She smiled. "Then maybe we need to go back to discussing our beach wedding?"

"I'm all about that. With one provision."

She raised her eyebrows in question.

"You let me eat first."

She looked toward the car. "Sure."

He grinned at her. "You stay and for God's sake, make yourself decent, you wanton, horny, young woman." He grabbed her again and kissed her. "I'll get the food."

"Deal," she said. "Damn. My T-shirt is totally wrecked." She pouted accusingly at him as she picked up the crumpled, dirty shirt he'd accidentally been standing on.

He threw her his T-shirt. "It'll look better on you anyway." He pulled on his jeans without doing them up and went to the car. She made sure he wasn't looking and then inhaled the scent of his T-shirt. "I saw that, you crazy stalker!" he yelled without looking around.

She laughed and pulled it on, along with her skirt. The panties were beyond saving.

They ate, laughed, and returned to base—only stopping for a fast, illicit kiss that she hoped no one saw.

They made plans for the following evening, after their night mission.

After dropping him off, she drove down the flight line—illegally—to her hangar. She needed to be near her Viper, to touch it. She wanted to marry the two remarkable highs—flying and being with Dex. She felt the same excitement with each. Like she'd already gotten her promotion and won the lottery on the same day.

Grinning, she opened the hangar door, just enough to slip in. Damn. The lights had been left on. That wasn't good form. Missy and her pilot, Lieutenant Colonel Francis Conrad, were supposed to be sleeping there that night. Their cots were against the wall, but no one had touched the sleeping bags rolled on top.

Eleanor looked at her watch. It was still early; maybe they'd be down later. Making her way to her aircraft, which was chocked in the back left-hand corner of the hangar, she noticed the rolling metal tool cabinet was open. She clocked it and shrugged it off. Maybe the crew chief had been in a hurry. She stopped short. A shiver rippled up the back of her neck.

No. Something wasn't right. No one in their crew would carelessly leave their tools out. Slowly, she swiveled around on the spot, looking for movement, anything that shouldn't be there. Unexplained fear fizzed under her skin.

There was no one there.

She put her hand on the fuselage of her aircraft and lightly walked around it, stroking it as she went. This time though—and for the first time—her gaze wasn't on the fuel intake, the rivets that held the canopy, the flaps. She could feel someone's presence.

She stood still again, trying to sense a movement in the air, the sound of breathing, anything really that would prove she wasn't being paranoid. Out of the corner of her eye, she saw something red. She spun around, and her heart rate jumped. It wasn't a person. It was a word.

Someone had written "Bitch" on the side of her canopy in lipstick. Goose bumps erupted over her body. Who would have done that? Munster? The TGO goons? Some other person she'd pissed off sometime? She couldn't believe it was Munster. Except he'd do anything to psych her out. This was Red Flag. Anyone could have wanted to psych her out of the exercise. To unnerve her somehow. Or to warn her off.

Prickles of unease flickered against her spine.

It was working.

CHAPTER FOURTEEN

Three hours into the night mission

Dex refused to use the words that would signal an emergency. Not again. He tried to level out his wings, but the aircraft kept fighting him. He couldn't understand it. He'd been through this in the simulator a hundred times. The aircraft always responded. "You stupid, bloody thing. What's wrong with you?" he muttered.

He went through his mental checklist, with his eyes glued to the display panels of his Eurofighter Typhoon. He'd started in a tailspin, and although he pulled out of it, all his controls—the rudders, the throttle, the flaps—were totally fucked up.

It was as if his own aircraft were fighting him for control. He tried to slow down, and the cockpit was filled with a loud Klaxon and the sterile, hated voice of Nagging Nora. *"Stalling. Stalling. Stalling."* But before he could react, the plane tipped down and throttled—almost as if it were correcting itself, only to then throw him back into his seat with the g-force of a sudden acceleration upward. Fuck.

He had no idea what was going on, but the thought that he absolutely couldn't crash a second plane and keep his career fucking raced out of his head.

Thank God he was over the desert. He tried to slow down, using the tiniest of adjustments. Just when he thought he'd figured out how to establish some kind of control, Nagging Nora screamed, *"Collision! Collision!"*

Frantically he looked around, swiveling to see what was out there, but before he saw anything, his plane lurched. As it staggered, the throttle juddering in his hand, another aircraft spun over him, also out of control by the looks.

Horror threaded through him as he saw it spin away from him, in the slow tailspin that he'd been in before he'd managed to climb out of it. As he watched, struggling to keep his wings level at the very least, the canopy of the other plane popped off. Jesus. The pilot was ejecting.

He tried to make contact on his radio, but all he found was static, as if his controller wasn't there.

Bile rose in his throat as he saw the pilot eject, rockets blasting under his seat as it pushed him into the sky. He watched until the parachute deployed. He hoped the poor bastard had been able to call Mayday and hadn't been met with the static Dex had.

Something was wrong. There was no good reason two different aircraft should have the same problem, in the same area, at the same time.

The Typhoon rolled onto its side, accelerating, increasing the g-force and distorting his vision. His body felt like a rock. He had a decision to make: land the fucker or bail out.

Every instinct told him to bail out, but he'd successfully landed a broken aircraft before.

Fuck his life, fuck his career, and fuck whatever was wrong with his plane. "Mayday, Mayday," a jerky voice came through his headphones. Was that him? Had he said that? Darkness speckled the edges of his vision. He fought the impulse to rip his mask off. He pressed his lips together. He tried to reach for the button that automatically orientated the aircraft should a pilot lose control, but the spin was so constant that he couldn't reach it. He took a deep breath and tried to figure out which way to reach to compensate for the spin. He found it and the plane righted itself immediately.

He had to get it down before it started acting up again.

He had no choice now. With a steely resolve, he lowered the landing gear and back throttled, using his flaps to descend quickly. The aircraft tried to speed up again, but his time he was ready for it.

After five minutes fighting with his beloved aircraft, he landed on the valley floor. His landing gear collapsed immediately and he skidded, out of control toward the hillside.

CHAPTER FIFTEEN

Eleanor opened her eyes to unimaginable pressure. Every bone in her body throbbed with a sharp pain, and she was convinced that her Viper was actually on top of her. What had happened? Where was she? She took excruciatingly tiny breaths while she forced her brain to take stock.

She'd punched out. Her aircraft had stopped responding. Had fought her for every maneuver. Where was she? Where was her plane? Oh God, she hoped it had crashed harmlessly into a mountain and no one else got hurt. She couldn't even remember which direction she'd been going in.

In…out. In…out. She tried to focus. They had been on their way back from the range. The exercise had finished. All teams had lost when the controllers had sent in a third-party team to disrupt both the Aggressors and the Blue Team. She'd been angry. Her plane sluggish.

Desperation seeped into her like sticky black oil. She'd nearly hit another aircraft—nearly caused them to crash. She hoped they'd managed to radio in for help. Her radio had been all static. She hadn't been sure anyone had heard her Mayday call.

The force of the ejection had rendered her unconscious almost immediately.

Thankfully.

The world looked strange to her, until she realized that she was on her side, her parachute flapping in the soft breeze wafting across the desert floor. She felt as if her spine were poking through the top of her back. Every breath hurt. Blinking hurt. She needed a minute, or maybe a week to figure out what she could move. She moved her foot at the ankle, up and down. Maybe it had been good that she'd been unconscious when she landed. Wait—she hadn't been unconscious. She remembered being able to pull her knees together and bend them. Then she'd passed out. Or was that a false memory?

The propellant that had ejected her was essentially a set of rocket boosters. She'd been a rocket man. She wondered if she would survive to change her call sign to that.

"Are you okay?" a gruff voice said.

Eleanor tried to open her mouth to speak, but it felt like somebody had punched her jaw. As she tried to formulate a word, she found all she could push out was a mumble.

"Eleanor? Jesus, is that you? Eleanor? Can you hear me?" The voice came nearer.

All she could do was groan.

Through her blurred vision, she saw him slump to his knees before her. She tried to ask where he'd come from.

What he was doing here. What the hell had happened to her. But she couldn't. It was all she could do to stay conscious.

"I've got this. I've got this," the voice said.

It didn't seem as if he was speaking to her; it felt as if he was speaking to himself, urging himself to move, to speak, to do something. All she wanted to do was go back to sleep. Her body refused to move; her brain refused to work. She welcomed the blackness seeping into the corners of her vision.

"Eleanor, stay with me," he said, pushing his fingers into her sternum.

She was sure it was Dex. But what was he doing here? Was she hallucinating? Was this all in her mind, tricking her into believing she'd been rescued?

She tried to pull away from his touch, it hurt so badly. But he continued to press until she heard three clicks. Her body slumped over onto her back. Oh. He'd removed her from her parachute.

"Urgh," she grunted. The collapse of her body onto the sand hurt like a bastard. Suddenly she longed for the comfort of her flight seat. She took a deep breath and moved her arm toward him, but all she grabbed was sand. Was it a hallucination? Was he actually there? Or was this just part of her brain malfunctioning like the rest of her body?

"It's okay. You're okay. We made it," he said. She closed her eyes for a second and felt her hair being swept back. It wasn't her hair. He had taken off her helmet.

"Okay, you need to tell me when something hurts. I'm checking you over."

She sighed and closed her eyes. But the breath she took hurt her ribs. She had never punched out before. She never imagined that she would ever have to punch out, and she knew she was in bad shape. About 50 percent of pilots who have to eject from their aircraft don't survive. She guessed she was lucky to be in the other 50 percent group right now. And thank God she'd managed to pull out of supersonic speed. Only one person had ever survived punching out at eight hundred miles an hour. And his legs had virtually been ripped off.

She felt his hands on her legs. Dex gently removed her boot and moved her ankle. It hurt, but clearly it wasn't broken. And then he did the same to the other one. Still no crazy pain. He ran his hands up her legs, pressing against the bone and digging his fingers into the muscles beneath.

"If this is your way of copping a feel...," she mumbled.

"Copping a feel? I think I'm rubbing off on you."

She wanted to laugh but instead she just spluttered, her mouth dry from the air she'd rushed through at two hundred miles an hour strapped only to her seat. "Water?"

"No." His hands were on her thighs now. He rotated her legs out from her hips. It hurt like she'd been horseback riding for sixteen hours, but nothing was broken. "I have some in my aircraft. If you feel up to it, we'll go and get it." He paused. "Or you can stay here and I'll get it."

She tried to swallow to moisten her mouth. "In my aircraft too," she said. "Whose is nearest?"

"Mine," he said. "It went down about half a mile from here. Yours went over that ridge." He pointed. "I'd say you have two bruised or broken ribs, but that's it. You were lucky." He paused. "I'm not imagining it, right? You did nearly crash into my aircraft, midair, didn't you?"

"Uh. Yes. Sorry about that. I had no control over my bird. She was fighting me more than you." She hoped he'd laugh, but he didn't.

He frowned. "Mine too. At first it was sluggish, and then it was overcorrecting my every move." Dex looked into the distance.

"Mine was sluggish yesterday," she said. And then she remembered everything. Her father, TGO, the lipstick on her canopy—which she had wiped off so no one else would see it. Munster maybe? Should she tell Dex everything?

With the diagnosis that he had just given her, she rolled over onto her stomach so that she could persuade her knees to let her stand up. Given the fact that she apparently only had two broken ribs, she tried not to groan.

"Let's go get some water," she said. "The pararescuers should be here soon. But that all depends on how soon they realize where we were when we ejected. It could be as long as an hour. My seat has a GPS. We should go find it."

She slowly stood up and tried to mitigate the furious spinning of her head. She wondered if she had a concussion.

She looked to where he said his had crash-landed. "Okay, let's go while I still have the energy."

They made their way slowly down to the wreckage of his aircraft. Dex was limping, but not as badly as she was, and she realized she should have asked him if he was hurt too.

By the time they reached the Typhoon, the sun had already started to dip. It had taken them about an hour to walk half a mile. Way longer than it should have.

Dex stopped about five meters from his aircraft wreckage and held her back from going forward. "Do you see any smoke?" he asked, squinting.

"No, nothing. You can't see?" she asked, looking at him properly for the first time. There wasn't anything noticeably wrong with his face.

"My eyesight is just a little blurry," he said.

He looked as if he was about to pass out.

"Sit there." She pointed. "I'll get your supplies."

He didn't argue with her, and that worried her.

He really couldn't see for shit. Ever since he'd come to after the crash and realized he was actually on the ground, and in one piece, he realized his vision had been seriously compromised. Maybe a detached retina, maybe a concussion? Probably a concussion for sure. Everything had ejected from his pockets and been flung around the cockpit as the plane had hit the deck. Bollocks.

As he watched her limping toward his aircraft, making slow progress in the way they had from her landing site, he wondered if she was considering the possibility that their aircraft had been sabotaged. More than one person seemed to have had a grudge against her, and by association, him too.

He shook his head. Maybe he was just being paranoid. But who wouldn't be? His second crash-landing in less than two years? His career was over he was sure.

His Typhoon was a mass of jagged metal, charred parts, and crushed dreams.

Dex shifted on the hard ground. Sure, it looked sandy, but it was hard rock underneath his arse. Couldn't even pretend he was on the beach. Then he heard something, and the discomfort he felt washed out of his mind.

It was the familiar sound of an aircraft engine. He held one hand over his bad eye and scanned the sky around the valley. It wasn't as if they were lost; everyone had to have known exactly where they were. Eleanor's ejection seat and his aircraft both had GPS trackers in them, so if they could lock on to their frequencies, they were golden.

The aircraft came into view. An American F-15. Its engines screamed in protest as the pilot throttled back to make a slow pass over their location. They were too far below to notice him waving, so the pilot waggled his wings to indicate he had noted their location. It was something.

"How're you doing in there?" he called out to Eleanor.

A muffled voice answered. "Okay. I can reach your flight bag, but it's stuck. I can get to it. I just need to get a bit closer."

"You need any help?" he said, not wanting to get up from his prone position.

"I'm fine," she said.

He heard another noise above them, almost like a swarm of bees. He looked up, but with his blurred eyesight, he couldn't pinpoint where it was coming from.

For a second he watched Eleanor again. Not that she was doing anything spectacular, but she seemed to have managed to crawl farther into the cockpit through the Perspex canopy. Nothing about that was strange, except her arse seemed to be wiggling at him. He shouldn't look. It seemed...wrong somehow. They'd survived a potentially fatal accident, and he was watching her arse. But he was a man, and he didn't have the energy left to ignore his instinct.

Distracted, he missed the buzzing getting louder. But now it had his full attention. He looked up and covered one eye with his hand again, getting better focus when he just used one eye.

In an instant, he recognized the sound and the sight of a drone. What was a drone doing out here? Dex thought this airspace was restricted. Maybe it was next-gen search and rescue? If so, he was pretty impressed at how quickly it was on-site. Maybe the F-15 had given them coordinates. But still, that felt pretty fast from being spotted to the launch and arrival of a drone.

He watched as it descended and hovered over the far ridge of the valley. He wondered if he should wave, but he suspected the operator would be able to see two crashed aircraft. The drone was probably checking out Eleanor's wreckage. It seemed to be circling around, no doubt filming the site. He wished he could tell the operator not to bother, that it was a write-off. He didn't think the insurance would be enough to buy a new aircraft.

He heard a crunch of metal and his eyes flew back to Eleanor. "Are you okay?"

"Yeah, I'm just trying to reach for this...," she said.

He watched her trying to shuffle in farther as if she were

trying to reach something. It was a good sign—it meant at least some supplies had survived the crash.

The drone flew away from the crash site of her aircraft over the ridge, and Dex assumed it would make its way back to them. But it didn't.

It flew away, maybe about two hundred fifty meters to the north, and then Dex could not believe his eyes as he watched a small missile drop from the belly of the drone. He rubbed his good eye and tried to focus on it with both eyes.

Just as he got a lock on the missile, it hit something he couldn't see. Seconds later, flames and a huge explosive cloud of debris blew above the ridge. The sound of the explosion hit his ears seconds later.

Did they just destroy the wreckage of Eleanor's aircraft?

Disbelief crossed wires with a thread of fear in his brain. His head snapped around to Eleanor and then back to the burning debris spitting up into the air and floating down. The drone was making its way to them.

"Eleanor! Get out here!" he yelled.

"Just a minute. I've nearly got…"

Fuck. The woman was going to be the death of him. He got up, ignoring his complaining limbs, and ran as fast as he could to the aircraft. He caught hold of her feet and dragged her out of the aircraft with all the strength he could muster.

She gave a small squeal as her front jagged along something sharp. "What the fuck are you doing?" she shouted. "That fucking hurt."

He grabbed her by her shoulders and pulled her upright. He winced as he saw blood staining the front of her flight suit. "Is it going to hurt as much as that?" He pointed up at the drone in the sky and then at the smoke and debris on the ridge.

"It just blew up your wreckage."

CHAPTER SIXTEEN

Red Flag commander Duke Cameron white-knuckled the railings that stood between the air traffic controllers and the people observing. The one word he hoped never to hear on his watch had just come over the microphone. He looked around the small room; everyone's eyes were on him.

"Someone tell me what's going on," he said in a loud voice.

Before anyone could answer him, and he was sure nobody wanted to, the voice repeated itself over the American frequency.

"Mayday..." Then the radio fell to pure static.

"Identify yourself, pilot," the controller asked.

Static buzzed over the mic.

"Who was that? I can't tell. Was that a British or an Australian accent?" Cameron asked.

"It came on the British frequency," an airman said from the corner of the room. With a degree of abstraction, Cameron appreciated the fact that the airman hadn't made an assumption about the nationality of the caller, only about the frequency he had used. In real life, however, he wanted to know for sure.

An RAF airman stood. "That sounded like Ironman, sir. Flight Lieutenant Dexter Stone." The airman was white, his lower lip trembling very slightly.

"Thank you." Cameron didn't know whether to be thankful or horrified that it was Ironman out there in difficulty. On one hand, no one could handle an aircraft better, and on the other hand, it was hard to imagine how he could recover from two emergency situations—mentally or career-wise.

Cameron's heart beat fast but his voice was steady, thank God. "Air controllers: What. Happened?"

"I got something, sir," a young airman said.

Cameron could see the airman was struggling to hear, and it was only then that he realized the chatter in the air traffic control room had reached an unbearable level.

"Silence!" he yelled into the room. Silence fell immediately.

"Airman. What are you hearing?"

"Sir, I hear a female pilot trying to make contact with the pilot on the British frequency."

Cameron's gaze slowly turned to his left. The only female pilot on a mission today was the general's daughter.

General Daniels, who was standing and observing the air traffic controllers, said nothing but turned his attention to the radar screen in the middle of the room. He didn't look happy, but he didn't look scared either.

"Put her on open speaker, airman," Cameron said.

For the sake of form, he asked the pilot to identify herself.

"This is Major Daniels, sir," she said, her voice steady but tense.

"Sitrep, Major?" Cameron asked.

There was a click, and then static once again.

"Is this a radio problem?" Cameron asked the controllers.

"Negative, sir..." More static interrupted the transmission.

"It's another frequency," the German controller said. "It's my frequency. Listen." He pushed a button and everyone heard Major Daniels.

"...unching out, repeat, I'm punching out."

"What is going on out there? Two incidents within seconds of each other? This is *not* happening," Cameron barked. Could this be a terrorist act? Why was she skipping frequencies?

There was nothing but static for a couple of seconds, and Cameron wanted to hit something. He hated having to rely on others to be his eyes, that now he had to focus more on budgets and safety records than the thrill of the mission. For the thousandth time, something in the back of his mind told him he'd made a mistake to take the promotion and essentially bench himself. Every cell in his body wanted to be out on the range.

"What the hell is going on out there?" Cameron repeated. "Do any other controllers have any other incidents on their wire at the moment?"

Everyone shook their head, still not meeting his eyes.

Static filled the entire room.

"What the fuck?" Cameron asked. "Do we have World War Two radios in here?" It was a rhetorical question; they had state-of-the-art digital, and digital backup, radios in the control room. There was no reason for any static to be on the wires.

"Ah, maybe it's sporadic E?" the airman on the Aggressor Squadron frequency suggested.

Cameron just glared at him. Sporadic E was the excuse radio controllers used when they were pretending not to hear someone. He wasn't amused. And then he remembered that Eleanor's father was still in the room.

"Sir—" he began.

The general held up his hand to silence him. The CEO of TechGen-One was whispering in his ear, one hand on the general's shoulder and the other on his arm. He seemed like such a nice guy. Genuine at least.

"Do you have comms with the either pilot?" Cameron asked the first airman.

"Negative, sir."

He took a chance and looked at the general again.

The general nodded toward the civilian. "Mr. Danvers has offered to send his elite search-and-rescue team. I'm reluctant to tell you they have many more resources than we do. His team is going to get these two pilots." Was his voice shaking? Of course, he must be worried for his daughter.

Nonetheless, Cameron frowned. "Sir. That's not protocol. Our pararescuers are here for a reason. They are here to train as well. It's amazing that TGO would offer, but we need to go get our guys ourselves. We can't trust our airmen to—"

The general interrupted. "I completely understand. But the deal we made with TechGen-One to fund Red Flag was that they had authority over operations. They need to train their teams too. I trust them, Commander." His mouth twisted a little. "I trust them with my daughter's life."

Cameron couldn't even begin to fathom how operational control had been given to a private company without reading him into the situation. He couldn't begin to fathom how he would write his report on this. Having a third party in on the rescuing of military resources, to include personnel, was unheard of.

But he couldn't argue with the general, and he only had scant information on the deals that were made in the background to make this Red Flag happen. In truth, he could have known more, but when he heard they had saved Red Flag, he was so relieved that he didn't consider what may have been given up in order to have TGO Industries step in. That was on him.

"Copy that, sir."

The general nodded, and Danvers made a call on his cell.

Cameron turned back to the air traffic controllers. "Anything?"

"Nothing from either, sir."

More static came over the speaker, and a new voice made contact. "ATC, this is Warbird 13. Do you copy?"

"Warbird, this is ATC," Cameron said over the speaker. Missy "Warbird" Malden was a breath of fresh air among this fuckery. She was always calm and responsible.

"We heard the transmission from Major Daniels. We located what looked like a downed aircraft in the valley to the west of Kawich Peak. Wasn't one of ours, though. We also think we saw a person outside the plane."

The knot in Cameron's stomach loosened just a little bit. That meant at least Ironman had managed to disengage himself from the aircraft, which was a good indication of life. "Roger that, Warbird."

Silence fell over the room. The general and Danvers spoke in low voices and then just left the room. The only person left in the spectator area was Casey Jacobs, the executive from TGO. She looked worried. Very worried. He could understand that; she'd been a Red Flag pilot herself. But her concern didn't look to him like a natural concern over the loss of pilots. There was something else.

He just had to find a spare moment to figure out what that was.

CHAPTER SEVENTEEN

What are you talking about?" Eleanor frowned at Dex.

"That drone." He pointed in the vague direction he thought the drone was in. "Fired a missile at your plane." He put his hand on her head to turn it to where dust was settling on the ridge. "The wreckage of your plane, at least."

Oh God. Maybe the crash had given him a serious concussion. "Are you all right?" she said in a gentle tone.

His facial expression told her that he couldn't believe she wasn't following what he was talking about.

"Dude. That drone blew up what was left of your aircraft."

"Dude," she mimicked him. "There's no way there would be a drone on-site, especially one with the capability to blow up an aircraft." She slung his bag over her shoulder and rooted inside for the bottle of water he said he'd packed. There was only one, though, so she hoped the pararescuers would pick them up quickly.

He jabbed his finger upward. "Listen."

She sighed and rolled her eyes, but to humor him she looked to the skies and concentrated. There was definitely a drone. She recognized the sound from being downrange. If she stayed still, she could hear it, but she couldn't see it against the bright sky. "What the…?"

Dex grabbed her arm and pulled. "Let's get out of here."

"I don't understand," she said with a frown.

"Please trust me." He released her arm.

She still hesitated.

"Okay, you can stay here, love, but I'm getting the fuck out of Dodge."

The buzzing of the drone intensified and Eleanor picked it up when it descended low enough in the sky to be seen against the gray rock. She figured it was a TechGen-One drone, maybe part of their new search-and-rescue capabilities that she'd heard about in briefing.

She watched its progress as a hand dug for anything else that might be useful in Dex's flight bag. But all thought of food disappeared from her mind as she watched the drone's cargo bay doors open. Her mouth dropped open. She had no words to explain what she was seeing. He was right.

Her legs started pumping before her brain had caught up. She craned her head as she ran and watched the missile leaving the drone. In disbelief, she saw it correct its course and aim directly at the wreckage of his aircraft.

What the fuck? Why would anyone…? Who had drones with a payload of missiles?

"Jesus!" she yelled.

Without looking around, Dex held his hand out to her.

For a second he looked like those perfect Instagram photos of a couple going into a new world or a new adventure. Not like somebody trying to escape a missile attack.

She took his hand but the instant her fingers touched his, a wave of energy pushed them over, snapping her head forward and completely disorientating her. Her mouth was full of sand, and the blast pushed every cubic inch of oxygen from her lungs. She tried to breathe, but she couldn't.

As blackness overcame her, her last thought was about the man whose hand was still in hers.

Dex woke up before Eleanor. He spat sand from his mouth and tried to lift his head. He couldn't. He felt as if it were strapped to the earth. Not to mention the fact that his brain felt like it was pulsing through his skull, like his head was too small to contain it.

It was not good.

He opened his eyes—at least they worked. Just not very well. He could see Eleanor's outline. She wasn't stirring but her hand was still in his. He released it and tried to dig his fingers into the ground to pull himself closer to her. It felt like it took an hour to move two inches. He was in serious trouble. He was sure a concussion on top of a concussion on top of a damaged retina probably wasn't going to speak well to his ongoing career as a pilot. Who would have thought he could crash another aircraft and walk away with fewer injuries than he had when he crashed the first one? Maybe he was just learning how to crash well.

He managed to roll one leg underneath him so he could

turn on his back. He had to get himself sorted. Lying on his back made him feel as if he was more in control. His lungs inflated better and if he really concentrated, he could stop himself from throwing up.

By moving his head very slightly, he saw Eleanor's water bottle peeking out from underneath her. He grabbed it with the hand that was in less pain and pulled it onto his belly so he could undo the top. He allowed himself one gulp before replacing the top and planting in the sand.

Come on, Dex. This is all on you. You've got to be strong. You've got to pretend this is a day at the beach. A cakewalk. A piece of piss.

Eleanor groaned, and his heart leapt. She was alive. It wasn't until that second that he realized the desperation he had been feeling was the unacknowledged thought that she had already died.

"Are you okay?" he asked, trying not to move his head too much.

She replied, but he couldn't hear her. He tried to shuffle closer so his ear was close to her mouth. "Say again?" he said gently.

"Do I fucking look okay?" she whispered.

He started to laugh, almost choked, ended up coughing and then groaning from the pain. After a second to compose himself, he said, "Do you want some water?"

She took a breath and nodded.

He grabbed the bottle and placed it to her mouth, tipping it to allow the water to trickle over her lips.

She stuck her tongue out to catch the water, and even

though he could barely see, it was enough for a tiny moment of rejoicing.

With concerted effort, he heaved himself up so he was sitting. His head rang, but through the noise, he heard the drone's return. "Shit."

"Quick, lie down," she said, tugging at his sleeve.

He already understood what she meant. Playing dead was their best option at the moment, although he wasn't sure if the drone worked on GPS locator or if it actually had a camera and an operator. He lay next to her, eyes closed, and waited for the drone to pass.

If he had been allowed to carry his weapon, he would have shot that sucker out of the sky.

When it passed, he sat up again. "You need an assist?"

"Nah, I got it." She pulled herself upright and grabbed the bottle of water. She took a couple of sips, then answered his question. "I saw the missile correct its path. Pretty sure that means there's a camera and an operator attached to it at some end."

That confirmed it: she was definitely inside his head, not just under his skin. He took a moment and then asked the obvious question. "This is an exercise, right? I mean, you didn't drag me into the middle of a drug war out here, or something?"

"Firstly, I didn't drag you anywhere, and secondly, I have no idea. There are not supposed to be drones out here. It certainly wasn't part of our mission brief, and I'm fairly sure both our governments would frown upon the wanton destruction of our aircraft and their black boxes."

Dex hadn't thought about it before, but he was fairly convinced that his black box information was automatically
transmitted on impact. It was a way of making sure nobody
would have to risk their life to get a black box in the middle
of the combat zone. He had no idea if the U.S. aircraft had
the same technology, and frankly, under the circumstances,
he wasn't sure he wanted to share any intel on his aircraft capabilities at the moment.

"So who did? Who has a vested interest in blowing up our
aircraft?" he asked. He took a breath and got to his feet. He
paused. And an idea unfurled in his head.

"It's not going to be anyone with a white hat," she said.
She stuck her hand out and he took it and pulled her to her
feet. She stood bent over for a second and groaned as she
stood upright. "The victories, I'll take them."

"Can you tell me this has nothing to do with the TGO
men who were hell-bent on grabbing you the other day?"

"I can't," she said baldly.

Shit. He looked around the barren valley. "So what's the
protocol here? Do you have search and rescue?"

"We have the best search and rescue. The pararescuers will
go through fire to get to us, wherever we are in the world.
So, this should be a piece of cake for them," she said. But her
voice had a tone of uncertainty about it.

"What aren't you telling me?" he asked.

She blew her cheeks out and looked around them. "Yeah,
we need to talk."

He rolled his eyes. "Why doesn't that surprise me? Come
on, let's find somewhere safe to wait."

"So where should we go?" she asked.

Logic would dictate they stay as close to the aircraft as possible so that they would be as easy as possible to find. But he didn't feel as comfortable doing that with the drone in the skies above them.

"If only I had a weapon, I wouldn't feel quite as vulnerable staying with the aircraft," he said. "I think we have a couple of options. We stay here and hope we're not sitting ducks, or we go find your seat and see if the radio's still working to contact somebody to see what's going on. At least report the fact that a missile took down our craft. There's a rock formation over there." He pointed to large boulders edging the bottom of the hillside. "Why don't we take cover over there and wait for your pararescuers? If they don't come within the hour, then we can go find your seat. I think it's about a mile away."

She nodded. "Sounds like a decent plan. Let's go."

About twenty minutes later, they reached the rocky outcrop, and after circling it they chose a place to sit that would give them some shelter but also wouldn't block the view of the valley.

"So, what's a nice girl like you…," he began, knowing full well she wouldn't let him finish.

She sat with her legs outstretched, her back against the rock next to him. Close enough to make him want to put his arm around her.

"I don't know exactly who was after me. My best guess is TGO. I overheard the CEO—Danvers—speaking with my father. They were saying things like *sanitized* and *share prices that would be worth billions*. I also got the impression that

TGO had arranged for my father to be at Red Flag this year. When I asked him about it, he just about lost it with me, shouting that TGO had shareholders in Congress and the cabinet."

It took every ounce of his willpower not to react, since he was pretty sure he knew what was coming next. He didn't say anything, just let her fill the silence.

"I think Danvers realized I'd overheard their conversation and tried to have those men pick me up or scare me into not talking. And then you got involved."

"Do you think they messed with our aircraft?" A bubble of anger grew in his stomach. He knew that was the only plausible answer, but he had to know if Eleanor could admit that her father had tried to get her killed. Or was at least complicit in it.

"That's the only thing I can think of. Why else would they use a drone except to destroy any evidence that the aircraft had been tampered with?"

He couldn't imagine what she was thinking. "Are you okay?"

She shrugged.

He snaked his arm around her shoulder and drew her closer, saying nothing.

"I don't believe my father wants me dead, but I do believe that he got himself into something with much higher stakes than he could have ever imagined. I never got on with him, especially after Mom left him for having an affair, but he's a patriot. I'm sure of it. I just…don't know what his part in this is."

She took a swig of water and then held the bottle up as if to measure how much was left. It was half empty. Yeah, half empty. He couldn't even bring himself to say it was half full. There was nothing lucky about today, not much to be optimistic about. Except he was alone with Eleanor. This wasn't exactly what he'd hoped they'd be doing on their next date.

"I think there's one more bottle," he said, taking the bag. "Until we know…" He looked at her and shrugged. "We'd better ration."

She didn't ask him, "Know what?" so she definitely knew what he meant. Right now, they didn't know anything for sure. There was nothing like being stranded in the desert to make you paranoid. And like the saying went: just because you're paranoid doesn't mean they're not out to get you. Up was down, night was day, and a drone had just blown up their aircraft in the middle of a secure military zone.

"Good thinking." Silence fell between them. It was a hell of a way to spend an evening. His mind kept searching for something he'd missed while he was still in the aircraft. What hadn't he done? What could he have done differently? What had they all missed in preflight?

Eleanor held up her hand in front of her eyes. It was shaking, but not in a normal "I nearly died" way. It was shaking uncontrollably.

He swiveled to look at her. Fear was etched on her face, her eyes alarmed, and her chin trembled. He grabbed her hand. "Don't. You've got this."

She opened her mouth to say something and her whole body started to shake. "I just lost my plane. I know I'm injured and I just can't tell where. And I don't know who sent that drone. I'm scared it might be the military. I'm even more scared that it could be TGO, or my father."

Dex had internalized everything she was feeling. If he were a better man, he would have been able to verbalize it also. But instead all he could do was try to take her mind off it. "You know, all that is pretty scary, but it's not as scary as your hair right now."

She huffed out a breath that could have been a laugh.

"And as bad as your hair is, it's still not as bad as you making me think I was a mai tai man the other night," he continued. What a ridiculously crazy night that had been. Dangerous and reckless—both things he thought he had left behind last year. Which he guessed made her a bad influence. Something he had been called pretty much every week from his sixteenth birthday until last year. It was nice for the shoe to be on the other foot for once. "So, answer me this, Eleanor: Do you usually pick up men you don't know and have your wicked way with them in a Las Vegas bar?"

Whether she realized it or not, her hands were steadying under this new line of questioning.

"Wouldn't you like to know," she said.

"Yes. I would like to know, very much. Because if I have to save your arse out here, I want to know that I'm at least special. I mean, I'm not going to risk my life for you if I'm just any other guy on the street."

"You think I pick up men every day?" Her tone had a very welcome edge of steel to it. This was more like the Eleanor he knew. Well, not that he knew her very well.

"Hell, if I looked like you, I would. Every night, and twice on Sundays," he said.

She laughed out loud. "Ha! That doesn't surprise me in the least. So, tell me, Dexter, do you pick up random girls when you're away from home?"

"I'm hurt that you'd ask that. Are you saying I couldn't pick up random girls at home too?"

"I figured that you'd have already been through all the women at home." She stretched out her legs and put her head on his shoulder.

"I have to admit, if I met a woman like you on every trip, I'd be shagging nonstop."

The thought of having her with him every night was turning him on. It was turning him on through his throbbing headache, through his broken ribs, and through his dodgy eyesight. And hell, he may not be alone with her for long again. Depending on how quickly the pararescuers found them, he might *never* be alone with her again.

"I'm going to keep you safe out here in the wilderness," he said in a mock-important way. "Only because you owe me a beach wedding."

Laughing, but not answering, he noticed, she reached both arms up and stretched. There were audible snaps as her spine expanded. She winced. "Do you think we'll be able to fly again?"

Well that was a splash of cold water. "I think you will be able to again. I mean, your injuries don't seem so bad. Even if they let me fly again, I'm not sure I'll be able to. My eye."

She started at my words. "Geez, I forgot. Let me look,"

she said. Her fingers were delicate, gentle, as if his face were one big bruise. Which it could have been as far as he knew. Her cool fingertips helped soothe the ache.

"I'm not going to lie to you, it doesn't look good. There's a ring of blood around your iris, and I have no idea what that means." She dropped her hand from his face, and he caught it in his. "Then again, I didn't see you before you got in your aircraft, so this could just be what you look like with a hangover."

He smiled even though it hurt his face to do so. "Well, I hate to say so, but I wasn't hungover this morning and I wasn't drunk last night," he said. He bit his lip to prevent a grin, and then assumed a serious face. "This could be our last night together."

She actually giggled. "Aha? You're going to war and this might be your last day on earth?" She rolled her eyes but didn't pull her hand away from his.

"Exactly. I'm an old beaten up combat veteran, sad, miserable—"

"You know those last two words mean the same thing, right?" she interrupted.

"...miserable, sad, desk jockey now. This was my last day flying probably. It's really the least you could do..."

She actually shrieked with laughter. She opened her mouth, undoubtedly to shoot him down, when they both heard the unmistakable sound of a helicopter. Close enough to make them both look up but obviously not close enough for them to be seen.

"I think this is the moment that we really need to think

about who is coming for us," he said. He didn't want to alarm her unnecessarily, but they needed to come to grips with the worst-case scenario.

Eleanor nodded. "If it's the good guys, I'll recognize them. If it's the bad guys…" She closed her eyes and shook her head as if to clear the haze of uncertainty from her mind. "Okay, let's go through this. It's the bad guys, isn't it?"

"Probably. I mean, is it normal protocol to send a drone to blow up a crashed aircraft?" he asked, holding her arm as she made to get up.

"No. And let's face it—nothing is protocol since TechGen-One took over." She took a breath. "I'm afraid I got you into this. Everything that has happened has stemmed from me overhearing a stupid conversation." She looked up with pain in her eyes. "I got you involved in this."

"No. Don't think that. Look, if the bad guys are gunning for you, you know you're doing something right. So shake it off. We need to make a plan," he said, taking her hand in his and squeezing it.

She nodded. "We have to assume our 'rescuers' are from TGO. We can't trust anyone until we get back…" Her words trailed off, and he knew she was deciding if she could trust anyone back on base, even.

"You can trust me," he said.

She gave him a half-smile, and he wondered if she would trust him if the situation was reversed. She barely knew him, after all. And clearly she was having the worst day of her life.

"All right then. We're agreed. Odds are these are the bad

guys. Your father is complicit, TGO is out to get us, and we need a motherfucking plan to survive."

There was silence for a minute and then she spoke. "I had no idea you Brits were quite so dramatic."

He laughed quietly. "Maybe I've been watching too many movies."

She grinned but didn't reply and he realized he was still holding on to her hand. He dropped his.

The sound of the helicopter was getting louder, but neither of them could see where they were coming from without leaving their hideout.

"We do need a plan," she said, turning a little so she was facing him.

"Already working on it."

Twenty minutes later, Eleanor was limping deliberately down the side of the ridge, her hands in the air, waving to the helicopter circling the wreckage.

She collapsed right at the very bottom of the slope, skidding in scree. She sat, as if she was unable to get up. The first thing she noticed was that the helicopter was not a Black Hawk, the type of helo the parajumpers generally used. But since she'd never seen the PJs deploy at Red Flag, she had no idea if that was normal or if they used the exercise to try out different equipment.

The helicopter landed fast. Four men jumped out—so far, so good. What wasn't so good was that they were carrying foreign weapons, dressed in black, and began their approach in a raid formation as the helo took off.

Shit.

She swallowed, took a breath, and then acted her part. "Hey, guys!" She waved at them again and then made to get up and fall over again as if she couldn't. She noticed that they stopped when she tried to get up, so she did it again.

And again. If her life weren't so in danger, she might have even enjoyed this game. She was trying hard not to look for Dex.

The men in black stopped moving as their leader held up a fist to them. They were about twenty meters away. "Where's the other pilot? The Brit?" the leader called.

She dipped her chin for a second, shook her head, and then tried to meet his gaze. "He didn't make it. The crash broke his neck." The guy was definitely American. And definitely not a pararescuer. An airman would have called her "ma'am" and asked for her rescue word to be sure they were rescuing the right person.

The lead guy looked back at the three behind him, and they exchange glances. She had a horrible idea that those glances were bad guy code for "this is easy. We only have to kill one woman."

Where the fuck were the pararescuers? Why were these guys hell-bent on getting rid of them? And, most of all, where the fuck was Dex? Had she made a mistake trusting a man she barely knew?

She made a struggle to get up, and this time she did manage to stand. She deliberately held one foot off the ground as if it hurt her.

Out of the corner of her eye, she saw Dex emerge from the

rock formation to her left and make his way behind the four men. Thank God.

She limped toward the men, eyes on the ground, purposely not noticing the lead guy hold up his hand to stop. She got halfway to him, groaning in pain, before he spoke.

"Stop right there. Stop!" he said, his hand still held out.

She looked up at him, eyes wide, as innocent as she could make them. Shit. It was the guy with long hair who'd tried to abduct her in Vegas. He'd never believe that she wouldn't be wary of him. It was now or never.

He raised his weapon, pointing it at her. She had to distract him.

She took a step closer. "What the fuck is this all about? Why do you want to kill me?"

He opened his mouth to speak, and as he did, she wrapped her hand around the end of his rifle and yanked it toward her, to one side. He was totally unprepared and stumbled forward, thrown off balance. As he fell, she kicked him in the solar plexus.

She couldn't get her hand back on his rifle, but she could get the gun he had carelessly put in a crappy nylon thigh holster. Who did he think he was? Lara fucking Croft?

She snatched it out of his holster, thumbed the safety off, and held the gun against the leader's head. "What is this about?" She looked up to the guy on her left. "Speak or I'll shoot him."

She watched, almost in slow motion, as he arced his own rifle up to take a shot at her. She shot him, and as he fell, the leader jumped up, both hands grabbing her wrist, fighting for the weapon.

In that moment Dex jumped the guy on the right, who was also bringing his weapon around. The leader punched Eleanor in the side of the head, and she went down.

She must have blacked out, as by the time she struggled to pull her head off the ground, the only two people standing were Dex and the leader.

Get up get up get up. She crawled onto her hands and knees but sagged with the effort. Her body would never be the same again, assuming they got out of this alive. She couldn't stand up, so she crawled over to where the leader had Dex in a headlock. She took a couple of breaths. *Come on, come on, you can do this.*

Literally the only thing she could do, the only thing that she had any power over, was her mouth. She leaned forward and bit the back of the leader's thigh. About the only area that wasn't covered in body armor. He screamed like a banshee, turned around, and kicked her. Everything went black. Again.

Dex looked at the detritus on the ground before him. Two dead, three knocked out—including Eleanor.

He fought every instinct he had to kneel over her, to touch her to make sure she wasn't badly injured. He had to protect them first.

He hog-tied the two men who hadn't died with wrist binders he'd found attached to a utility belt on the lead guy. It gave him pause, though: Why would the guy have ties if he was supposed to kill them?

Once that was done, he grabbed Eleanor by the tape at the back of her flight suit, lifted her shoulders off the ground, and dragged her away from the scene as fast as he could go. As soon as they were out of sight of the men who could come to at any minute, he gently laid her back down.

"Eleanor? Come on, love." He gently tapped the top of her arm, urging her to regain consciousness. It was concerning that she was still unconscious, especially given that two concussions in a short space of time could lead to serious issues. And their ability to evade their pursuers would be dramatically curtailed if it was just him and an unconscious Eleanor.

He quickly checked her body over for other injuries. She seemed okay, but the bigger concern was her brain. And he was sure she wouldn't be happy thinking that he was worried about her brain.

One of the men he'd hog-tied groaned. They needed to get farther away from them. When the helo returned, he and Eleanor needed to be way over the ridge and hidden away. Dex planted his feet, grabbed her right arm, and pulled her over his back.

His ribs shrieked in agony as he took his first step. They just had to get somewhere safe, somewhere they could stay hidden, somewhere he could check out the bag that he'd stolen from one of the bad guys. Waste not want not.

He tried to walk as smoothly as he could, but with his ribs and his hip now complaining with every step, he was worried he was jolting her poor brain more than was healthy.

He estimated that he'd walked about three-quarters of a

kilometer around the base of the hill where they'd been hiding. Now they just had to hide again.

He was about to put her down and take a rest when she coughed and moaned and then made puking noises. Awesome.

He put her down and shifted out of the way, holding her waist.

"What the...?" she said before throwing up.

Definitely a sign of a concussion. "I know you feel like shit, love, but d'you think you can make it up there before you show me more of your lunch?" he asked, pointing to a pile of rocks up the hill.

She took a red and yellow bandanna from her pocket and wiped her mouth. Without saying anything, she looked at where he indicated, took a deep breath, and nodded.

"Let's go, before your body changes its mind." He motioned for her to go first, so that if she fell he could catch her. This had to happen quickly. The helicopter would come back, especially if they had no word from the people it left behind.

As they climbed, he tried to figure out why the helo had left. Presumably it had to go back to base—or wherever it had come from—to claim that it had found nobody. So, how were those guys supposed to get back?

He put his hand on Eleanor's arse to give her an assist up the hill. She didn't say anything, didn't swipe his hand away, didn't thank him. Nothing. As short a time as he had known her, he knew this was not a good sign.

Just below the top ridge, there was a huge pile of rocks

with gorse growing out of the cracks. "Just there. Sit down behind those." Happily, the rocks and gorse hid them better than he had imagined from the base of the hill. There was a little more room to stretch out, and with rocks on one side of them and the peak of the ridge on the other, he figured they could stay fairly well hidden. Unless somebody literally stumbled across them, they wouldn't be found.

Eleanor sat against the rock with her legs straight out. Her head banged back onto the rock and she groaned.

"You're going to kill yourself if you're not careful. Hold on a second." He unzipped his flight suit, pulled it down to his waist, and took off the brown T-shirt underneath. He folded it into a rough cushion and put it behind her head. "Look at me," he said, crouching in front of her.

"Do I really have to?" she said with a painful-looking grin on her face. But she opened her eyes anyway and looked at him.

He moved closer and tried to see her pupils. Her focus seemed okay. "Tell me exactly what hurts right now."

"Everything?" she said. "I'm serious. The pain in my head is making it hard to feel pain anywhere else."

Very quickly he pressed into her stomach, pressed her collarbone and across her shoulders, squeezed her waist, and ran his hand down the bones in her legs. "Anything?"

She closed her eyes and shook her head.

"That's something, I suppose." He sat opposite her and dragged the bag he'd stolen from the lead guy in front of him. He pulled out the four sidearms he'd also taken and set them on a rock.

"Give them to me," Eleanor said quietly. "I'll check the mags."

He passed them over and continued unpacking the bag. He already saw that there was one two-liter bottle of water in the outside pocket. He had a new appreciation for the man who tried to kill them as he pulled out the things from the bag. A map, compass, sleeping bag, protein bar, first-aid kit, an empty water canteen, and a book. He looked at the spine. "*How to Win Friends and Influence People*. I don't think he was taking any of the lessons in this book to heart."

She snuffled a laugh. "Any drugs?"

"None that I found. You know what else I haven't found? Any kind of ID. There was nothing on his body, nothing traceable in the bag. Except maybe the weapons." It was becoming pretty clear. It was just he and Eleanor against whoever was out here trying to kill them.

Eleanor winced. "It was the guy who tried to throw me in front of a limo that night in Vegas. TGO, I think."

"You never mentioned that before," he said, trying not to grit his teeth.

"But we know now. TGO is behind our aircraft malfunctioning and an obvious attempt on our life. I just don't know how or why."

"Me neither," he said slowly. "Do you think there's something here? Something on the ground that messed with our systems? It seems random that the same symptoms occurred in two different aircraft with different systems."

"Maybe, but when I first noticed the anomaly with my controls, I was about three miles from here. So, something might have a huge range, which would be incredibly dangerous…I just don't know. It's possible I guess." She sat up, pulling the T-shirt from behind her head. She twisted it between her hands. "Maybe it's mobile?"

"I don't know. I've never heard about any weapon like that. Like an EMP device, but it only affects avionics and not all electrical circuits?" He thought for a moment. "What we're saying is that someone did something to mess with our controls, and for some reason they felt as if they needed to destroy our aircraft and then kill us. Why would that be?"

Eleanor cleared her throat. "I'm pretty sure it's because I overheard the conversation between Danvers and my father. I'm sure active-duty generals aren't allowed to own shares in a company they're actively giving business to. And if that influence goes up high into government, who knows what they'll do. And I'm really sorry…really sorry. But they're probably targeting you because you helped me in Vegas, and I'm sure they think I told you what I knew. Which I guess I have." She paused. "I really don't know. It seems farfetched, doesn't it? I'm sure if my brain was working properly, and I was able to put a hundred forty-two and a hundred forty-two together to get two hundred and…" Her voice trailed off and her eyes closed again.

"Eighty-four," he said quietly. He was torn between wanting her to sleep and being concerned about her falling asleep because of her concussion. Not that it mattered that much. If memory served him, it was okay to let her as long she could hold a conversation. And despite not being able to add a hundred forty-two and a hundred forty-two, she seemed okay. He just needed to sit and think about how to get them out of the desert in one piece and how to protect themselves against the powerful people in America.

Come to Red Flag, they'd said. It will be a great experience. It will set you up for the rest of your career.

Fuckers.

He was going to let her sleep, wake her in half an hour. Maybe in that time he could come up with a plan. He opened the map they'd found and saw they appeared to be sixty miles away from base. But if he remembered the small laminated map in his cockpit, missions were taking place just north of where they were, where he had tried to bomb the convoy the previous day. That meant they only had to get to the mission site by morning to possibly be seen by one of the Red Flag military aircraft in the morning. It also meant walking in the opposite direction, away from the base. That may also give them the cover they needed. If someone was still searching for them, everyone would be looking between the crash site and Nellis.

They were going to have to start rationing the water. He closed his eyes and went to his happy place. His cottage in the north of England. His dog, Winston, who was being looked after by the neighbor. If he were being honest, he had a good life, whether he was flying or not. He just wanted to stay alive to enjoy it again.

What about Eleanor? He opened his eyes and gazed at her. He wondered what her life was like, wondered what she'd be going home to after this exercise. Would she fly again? Would she qualify for the Saddle Club? Would she like Winston? His home? Would she want to see him again after this, or would she want to forget everything? He wouldn't totally blame her.

He wanted to brush the hair out of her closed eyes, reach into her dreams to reassure her. But he didn't dare disturb her. Instead, he stretched his leg alongside hers and pressed it against hers. He hoped it might comfort her in her sleep, because it sure as hell made him feel better. A small smile kicked at the side of his mouth as he remembered her giving him his "loser patch." She'd have one now. They'd be a little family of losers.

He wondered if there was a double loser patch for him. Then he slept.

CHAPTER EIGHTEEN

Major Missy "Warbird" Malden had never actually spoken to a three-star general before. Nor the CEO of a military contractor. And today really wasn't a good time to do it. But there she stood, at attention in the general's office, with her first in command, Lieutenant Colonel Francis "Freak" Conrad at her side.

The CEO of TGO stood behind the general. She didn't remember his name, and he wasn't introduced to them, but she recognized him from the initial safety briefing in the auditorium.

Conrad stood close to her, almost touching.

They'd flown together for four years. Not every day, because they both flew with other people too. But when they did, they rocked the skies. No one could beat them. She was his weapons officer and flew the backseat of the F-15 they shared. She wondered if he could feel the tension radiating through her body.

"Major. Colonel." He looked between them. "I don't need to tell you that this is not the time for silence."

Still at attention, she did nothing but stare over his shoulder at the map behind his desk. She wondered whose career she could save—if any. A month ago she would have thrown herself under the bus for him. Now she wasn't so sure.

The general continued. "My daughter's plane is missing. Presumably crashed."

"I know, sir." Her voice trembled. She was scared for Eleanor and could not believe that a pilot with her ability had just disappeared along with her aircraft during a training exercise. She was also scared for another reason.

"As I said, this is not the time for silence," the general said.

He certainly didn't seem worried or concerned about his daughter. She couldn't imagine growing up with a father like that. Missy wondered for a second if that's why Eleanor took such risks, was such a daredevil. Maybe she was trying to get her father to show something—anything.

Conrad, to the right of her, was struggling to decide what to say. She hadn't been his second for four years without knowing what was going through his mind at any given time. It was why she was good at her job.

"Okay, let's start with the basics. You both told Sergeant Cripps that you were sleeping in the hangar last night."

Missy tried hard not to flash her eyes toward Conrad.

"I need to know what you saw that night." The general paced in front of his window. "I need to know if anyone touched her F-16."

"No, sir. We didn't see anything," she said.

"Here's the thing, Major. If you didn't see anything, maybe you did something yourself. Or maybe you saw the lieutenant colonel do something?"

She'd seen him do a lot last night. "No! Absolutely not! How could you..." Her words faltered when she realized that she shouldn't be speaking to a general like that.

Conrad came to her rescue. "Missy and Eleanor are friends. How could you suspect she—or I—would damage her aircraft? Either deliberately or accidentally?"

"Because there's no other explanation!" the general roared. "Eleanor and"—he flipped open a file on his desk—"Flight Lieutenant Dexter Stone are the best pilots in their squadrons. The only thing that could bring both of them down would be sabotage."

This was it. Her eyes fluttered closed in resignation. She was going be fired and probably sentenced to at least two years at Leavenworth. She would be lucky to get away with a dishonorable discharge. She deserved worse. Emotion fizzed in the back of her throat, and she willed herself not to cry. She'd let Eleanor down, and she would have to live with that her whole life.

"Sir. If you gave us hangars that were secure, your pilots and crew would not feel as if they had to sleep in their hangars." Conrad's voice was steely.

The general stopped pacing and glared. Missy averted her eyes. "Is that really your point, Colonel? My daughter could be dead, and you're complaining about the lack of a lock?"

Don't answer. Don't answer him. She tried to get Conrad to hear her silent voice as he had a thousand times before.

"Yes, I am, sir. A lock would prevent sabotage, wouldn't it? It would prevent accidents from happening. Knocks, dings on the aircraft?" Was he going to sacrifice himself for her? No, that wasn't it, not really. For all her ability to anticipate his every move, his strategies, his actions, she could not figure out why he was deliberately antagonizing the general.

She wasn't going to let him take the fall for this.

She stepped forward. "There was someone else in the hangar yesterday. Some civilians. I could point them out if you like. They even had a golf cart in there. But you know that, don't you? Eleanor told me she'd spoken to you about it."

The general paled and his gaze darted to the head of TGO. "She told you about our conversation?"

"Yes." She could feel her face flushing. "Of course she did. We're colleagues *and friends.*" She placed an emphasis on the last words, so he'd understand that she wouldn't hurt a friend.

Instead of calming down, the general's hands started to shake. He dropped the pen he was holding and snatched it up again as if he were embarrassed that he'd dropped it. The CEO of TGO put his hand on the general's shoulder. She would think that he was comforting him, but his expression wasn't one of comfort. Maybe he was the type of man who didn't know how to emote. She sneaked a look at Conrad, who was frowning.

"I simply don't believe you. It feels as if Red Flag is under attack, and the only way that could happen is an inside job. There's no other explanation," the general said. Shock stopped her thoughts from forming coherently. What had they done?

"You two are confined to barracks. You will not see each other; you will not talk to anyone, except for the investigators I will be sending to find out what your involvement is. We can leave no stone unturned."

Two MPs barreled into the office, their hands on their sidearms.

"They're under house arrest." The general sat behind his desk and opened a file as if he had already forgotten they were in the room.

As they were escorted from the general's office, she saw Conrad looking at her. His expression both distraught and determined. She tried to smile, but her chin wobbled as she did so.

He frowned, but as he turned to go with one of the MPs, his thumb grazed against the back of her hand.

She closed her eyes for a second. No, she couldn't get sucked in again.

They were responsible for Eleanor's aircraft being sabotaged. And that knowledge burned a hole in her stomach that may never go away.

CHAPTER NINETEEN

When Eleanor awoke, dusk hung in the air and a bare line of light illuminated the top of the hill they were on. She shifted to give some relief to her backside against the stone. She wondered again why the pararescuers hadn't come for her. Every sortie, every mission she had ever undertaken in her career had been embarked on with the knowledge that if worse came to worst, the Air Force pararescuers would be there for her. It was an unspoken deal. You put your life on the line, and someone was guaranteed to come for you. That they hadn't come was like finding out Santa wasn't real.

She looked at her watch, pressing the button that illuminated the dial. It was 6:00 p.m., time for the night missions to start preparing to leave Nellis. She wondered if they could get their attention somehow, but even in her desperation, she realized how remote a chance it was that the mission would come anywhere near them. Or that the pilots would be at the right altitude to see a signal from them. Not that she and

Dex had a signal. No flares, no glow stick, no nothing.

They could set fire to something, but that would just as easily bring the bad guys—whoever they were—to their door.

She looked across at Dex. When he wasn't talking, he was beautiful. Like a carved statue in a museum. It was so weird—the first man she had slept with in eight years, a hit-it-and-quit-it proposition, turned out to be the man she was on the run with. Maybe that was karma telling her that one-night stands weren't for her.

Or maybe that he is the one for me?

Dex stirred. "Awww…You look like sleeping beauty," she told him.

"That's what Mum always said," he replied. He took a deep breath and stretched his arms above his head. "How long have you been awake?"

"About five minutes. It's just after six."

He nodded. "How's your head?"

"Settling down into a dull thump. Nothing worse than a hangover, really." She shrugged.

"I hear you. Drink some more water. It will help your brain recover." He handed her a bottle, but she didn't take it.

"We need to ration it. We have no idea how long we will be here now."

"Does that mean you don't have a plan yet? What, were you just wasting those five minutes that you were awake before me?" He grinned.

"Actually, I do kind of have a plan, but you're probably not going to like it."

He nodded. "Go on."

"I want to head north. The drop zone is there for tomorrow's missions. If we could do something to attract their attention, we may get some legit help. If the Ospreys are flying tonight, they could even land right there and pick us up."

He paused for a moment, smiled, and nodded. "Sure. That makes sense. No one is likely to look for us going away from the base."

"I just want to get back to tell everyone to shut down TGO. If they're all bad guys, what are they doing to our systems, our other aircraft? They had virtually unlimited access to all coalition aircraft and systems. That's the scariest thing. It's worth dying for."

Dex smiled again. "Yes, it is. But let's try to stay alive."

She shook her head and met his eyes. "They said whatever they were doing was 'sanitized,' and I'm beginning to think that doesn't mean they're using hand wipes."

"I think we know that. I think we know they mean us, or anyone who gets in their way. But we've got an objective now. Are you up for it physically? It'll be a fairly long walk."

She nodded. "Of course I am. And if we happen to pass my aircraft, I want to try to get my hands on the flight recorder. It should have survived the blast. If someone hasn't already taken it."

"It's a good thought, but…"

"Also, my favorite lipstick was in my fireproof flight bag." She pressed her lips together to stop herself from grinning.

"What we're looking at is a long walk if we use the safety

of the hillside ridges to hide ourselves or a slightly shorter walk if we use a compass and walk directly across the basin," Dex said.

"Yeah. I vote for the longer route. We don't know who might come after us in the middle of the night. Besides, we need to find somewhere we can rest if we need to." Even though she'd just woken up, she was tired. Very tired. And although she was up to start walking right now, she didn't know how long she would be useful.

Dex watched carefully, as if he knew what she was thinking. "Are you sure you're up for this?"

She wanted to say no. She really wanted to stay right where they were and sleep. Leaving the safety of their hideout did not sit well with her. But this wasn't just about her; it was about the next pilot who had to bail out of an aircraft because someone had messed with it. This was about someone having access to all the aircraft on base. "Yes. I'm up for it."

"It's the right thing to do. You're right." He looked up the sky, which was fast becoming dark blue. A couple of stars were already out. "I haven't heard any aircraft, so it wouldn't surprise me if they suspended the exercise for the night."

"What happens if they suspend the exercise tomorrow too?"

"I have to believe there are good guys and bad guys. We fought the bad guys and won, for now. And if they send more, we'll beat those too. I think the good guys have yet to come, and when we get back to base, we'll understand why." His voice was reassuring. His words were not.

"In all honesty, I think I have two useful hours left before I'll need to sleep," she said.

He hesitated for a second and smiled. "Me too. We'll go as far as we can, then stop to rest."

She pushed herself up and stretched. Grabbing one of the handguns they had taken from the bad guys, she applied the safety and slipped it into her thigh pocket.

CHAPTER TWENTY

Red Flag commander Duke Cameron paced his office. This couldn't be happening. The last Red Flag exercise of his career was already a disaster, and two pilots were missing, presumed dead.

Two of the exercise's best pilots. He paused and looked out the window. There were miles of parked aircraft. Against everyone's wishes, he'd suspended the exercise until Major Daniels and Flight Lieutenant Stone were found. He would feel a lot better about this if the pararescuers were out looking. But General Daniels had authorized the military contractor to take search and rescue, and to Cameron's mind that was the worst decision he'd ever made.

Now that the general had put Malden and Conrad under house arrest, it felt like he—the commander here—had no fucking idea what was going on. It was like ghosts were here. *Ghosts. Or spies?*

Casey Jacobs strode into view below his window. A reluctant smile twitched at the edge of his mouth. He remembered a Red Flag long ago when she was the ballsy pilot no one could take their eyes off of. He had wanted her so badly back then, he could barely keep it in his pants. But as always, she had been nothing if not professional.

Oh yeah, he'd seen her looking at him a couple of times, and he was sure she had seen him looking her, but they'd barely even said hello to each other.

He watched as she walked across the flight line, smiling as she passed pilots and crew. Then she stopped dead in her tracks and patted her pockets. Eventually she pulled out a phone and looked at the screen. She looked around, hesitated, and then held it to her ear. She frowned, the lines on her forehead visible under her red bangs. That was interesting. What was she hiding?

She suddenly started to shout. He couldn't hear a word she was saying, but she was poking at the air with her forefinger and actually stomped one of her feet. He wondered who was on the other end of the line. A lover? A work subordinate?

And then she pulled the phone away from her ear and looked at it in disbelief. Her mouth fell open, and she looked around as if worried that somebody had overheard.

Duke stepped back from the window but kept his gaze focused on her. She dialed another number and waited for the call to be picked up. She started to speak, but again, her mouth dropped open. He could lip-read her reply. *"Are you kidding me?"*

His eyes narrowed. What was going on down there?

Then he actually heard her shout, albeit muffled. "I won't let you get away with this!"

The whole conversation was interesting. So was the timing. His two missing pilots had been out of contact for five hours now. Not even the surveillance aircraft had picked up any sign they were alive, just wrecked aircraft. They only had Major Malden's word that she'd seen someone alive down there when they'd flown over the crash site. And now both she and Conrad were in custody and under suspicion of sabotage, or impeding their investigation, or something that had the general concerned.

He picked up the phone and called the number from the card Casey had given him earlier. From the side of the window he watched as she took the call.

"This is Duke Cameron. Would you mind coming up to my office?" he asked.

Again, she pulled the phone from her ear and looked at the screen, as if she was wondering what to do. Why did she have to wonder?

"Of course. I can be there in five minutes," she said.

"Perfect. See you then." He hung up the phone.

She hesitated on the tarmac, looking around her as if someone could save her from having to talk to him. His suspicion grew. She waited an eternity before slipping her phone back into its pocket and heading toward the building.

He sat back at his desk and opened Eleanor's file again and looked at the photo that was clipped to the inside page. *Where are you?*

In any other situation, he would have gone out himself to

look. He had an idea that there were a lot of people downstairs who would do the same, if they weren't under strict orders to stay on base. Lockdown was a bitch. But he understood why the general had given the order. Without knowing what was going on, it was better to keep everyone safe on base.

There was a knock at the door.

"Come in," he said.

Casey came in, ruffling a hand through her hair. Worry was still etched around her eyes, but he smiled at her and with his eyes told her to take a seat.

"Been a long time since we've seen you at Nellis," he said.

The worry faded, and the smile touched her eyes. "I was so excited to hear I was going to come back here—even though of course I wouldn't be able to fly. But…"

"I know. I'd like to say we were doing everything we can find them, but right now that should be your line. What progress has your search and rescue made?"

She shifted in her seat and his gut told him that she was uncomfortable with the question. But she leaned forward as if eager to reply. The two actions didn't make sense together, but he let her speak.

"As far as I can tell, they've sent three sorties to comb the area where the wreckage is. One crew came back, not having found anything, and while they were refueling another took off. That's all I know."

"They found no signs of any personnel? Not even bodies?"

She smiled. "I assume not, or they would have reported it. That's good news. At least, as Mr. Danvers told me, it's good news unless they're injured somewhere."

He nodded.

"Why is TGO determined to do the SAR on this? If you were a pilot out there right now, would you want a private contractor, or would you want the pararescuers to come get you?"

She looked at his hand, and he realized he was tapping a pen on the desk. He put the pen down and remained silent, hoping for an honest answer from her.

"TGO has the best SAR teams in the industry, with the best technology." She spoke with the firm, clear voice. No hesitation, or doubt.

Maybe he was barking up the wrong tree, or maybe his frustration had him seeing bandits wherever he looked. But something about her interested him. Her eyes almost pleaded with him, but he couldn't trust himself to decide what they were pleading for. One false step, and he'd be in Minot, North Dakota, managing a supply chain.

"Let's get together later at the officers' club. We can grab a bite to eat. Catch up." He wasn't actually sure if he wanted to catch up or grill her about TGO.

She stared at him for a second, as if weighing her options. It was a strange pause. "I'd like that. What time?"

"Seven?" He looked at his watch.

Suddenly her face animated into a beautiful smile, a smile full of hope and joy. "It's a date!"

He swore that his heart stuttered at her words. Man, but he had to get a grip here. He wanted to find out more about TGO and their rescue efforts. Not that seeing her dressed in a black high-necked sweater and tight black jeans with cowboy boots interested him at all.

He wondered if he was kidding himself. He wondered if this was so out of line, it was on a whole other page. *Do you want to grill her about her employer? Or do you want to kiss her until she moans—like you fantasized about all those years ago?*

"I'll see you there," he said, standing.

She held out her hand. "Sure. Good to see you again."

He took her warm, small hand in his and resisted the urge to stare into her eyes.

As he watched her disappear along the corridor, he sat down.

Damn, this was a bad idea.

He swiveled his chair to look out the window again, with a smile playing on his face.

And then he realized she hadn't answered the question he had asked her about her own preference for SAR. All she had done in response was quote a line from a TGO brochure. He stared at the files on his desk, unseeing.

He was going to get to the bottom of this.

CHAPTER TWENTY-ONE

Eleanor and Dex had walked for about an hour, hugging the foothills, trying to stay invisible against the rocks. He pretty much knew this was a fool's errand. If her plane existed at all after the missile strike, it would be a mangled piece of metal. He doubted anyone without specialist equipment could get the flight recorder, but sometimes having a tangible goal, no matter how unlikely, was a good way to get you through an otherwise hopeless situation. At least they didn't have to make a detour. Her Viper, whatever was left of it, had been directly en route to the combat range. He hoped he could get them through this. He hoped she would let him get them through this.

"What are you thinking?" she asked in the silence.

"Oh, you don't want to know," he replied, hitching the backpack farther up his shoulders.

"Well, now I do," she said.

He grinned in the fading light. "So, I was thinking, does

Dexter Ironman Stone-Daniels sound weird? Maybe Dexter Ironman Daniels-Stone?"

She gave a small laugh, which was reward enough. "Getting ahead of yourself much?" she said.

"We could have a kid called Cold Stone-Daniels."

She giggled. "I'm not calling my son Cold. Besides, Cold Stone is the name of an ice cream store."

She put a hand on his shoulder to stop him. "I need a break."

He nodded, slipped the backpack off his shoulders, and handed her the bottle of water. He watched her as she drank from it.

"How did you get your call sign?" she asked, handing the water bottle back to him.

"It's a long, heroic story. I'm not sure I have time to do it justice. But there were lives at risk, babies rescued…basically the world was saved. You can thank me later." He screwed the cap back on the water and put it on the rock between them. "What about yours?"

She shrugged. "Ditto."

"No, seriously," he said, hoping she wouldn't press him on Ironman.

She sighed and rolled her shoulders. "We were called in one day in training. It was a drill, but I'd been working out in black yoga pants and a yellow and black striped workout top. They called me Bees, but after they flew with me, they changed it to Bees Knees."

"I'm not surprised. You've got a gift," he said.

"How do you know?" She turned to him, a quizzical expression on her face.

He sighed. "I'm fairly sure you nearly killed me on my first mission, and I'm certain that I killed you on my second mission."

"That was you?"

"You mean, was I the one who you flew out of the sun at? Yes, that was me. And it was also me who ambushed you from behind." He raised his eyebrows, realizing the double meaning of what he'd just said.

She grinned. "You've done that more than once."

"Why, yes, yes, I have." He pulled her to him, suddenly needing her closeness again. Her lips were warm against his. At the touch of his tongue, she opened her mouth under his and he was flying into the hot sun. Heat rose through him like mercury in a thermometer. Somewhere in the back of his mind, he knew this was the wrong place and the wrong time. But she was so right. Right for him in every way possible.

I'm not going to let her get away. And the alien thought didn't even surprise him. Why would it? She could battle with him toe-to-toe, wit for wit. She understood his lifestyle; hell, she lived his lifestyle. And her mind moved as fast as his did. Of course they should be together. The revelation felt easy, like it had been there his whole life, but only now he was able to pull back the curtain to see what was behind. And it was Eleanor.

She pulled back an inch from him and gazed at him. "You're very peculiar," she said.

"I'm not arguing with you at all, but how so?" He didn't care as long as she was looking at him with the naked desire she was showing on her face.

She just smiled. "How did you get your call sign?"

He sighed. "One of the guys in my old squadron was getting married, so we threw him a stag night...As it turned out, I was the one left naked at the end of the night. Stark naked." He raised his eyebrows again to see if she'd make the connection.

She frowned and then nodded, stifling a laugh. "Tony Stark. Iron Man. Saving the world, huh?"

"Look, you don't know what might have happened if that lovely policewoman hadn't escorted me back on base..." He leaned away to avoid a punch, but she just shook her head.

There was silence between them for a few moments. He picked up the water bottle, a little concerned about how long they would be out here and how long the water would last.

"Do you need to take a knee?" he asked.

"Man, from what you were talking about, I thought *you* were going to take a knee," she replied. "No, let's press on. It'll get tough when the sun disappears completely. I think we'll have to stop then."

"Roger that." He estimated they had about another twenty to thirty minutes of good light left if they were lucky.

"Wait." She grabbed his arm and looked toward the hill to their right. What had she heard? "Do you hear that?"

He couldn't hear anything, but since he couldn't see an awful lot either, he was going to have to rely on her. "What do you hear?"

"Water." She frowned. "That can't be possible, right?" Without waiting for an answer, she started scrambling up the scree.

"No. That's not right; we're in the desert. Come back." He spoke to her as if she were a child.

"Stop being a dick and come with me." She didn't even look behind her.

He sighed, grabbed the backpack, and followed her, fully prepared to take the piss, once she realized she was wrong.

"Oh my God," she said, abruptly coming to a halt near the top of the hill.

He climbed after her, and as he crested the peak, he saw what had halted her in her tracks. It looked like a huge ten foot by ten foot blast hole in the rock, filled with swishing water. "What is it? A tarn?"

"I don't know what a tarn is, and I don't care. It's water, and we need water."

Water didn't magically appear from the desert, usually, and that concerned him. Nearly all the lakes on the military range were dry or salt flats. "Okay, why don't we rest here for the night, and we can get an early start. And we can figure out where this water came from and if it's safe to drink."

He dropped the backpack, pulled out the map. He opened it once again and put a mark where he thought they were.

Before he'd finished folding it up again, he heard a splash. He jumped up, wondering if she had fallen in. But all there was to see was her flight suit and T-shirt and boots and socks on the edge of the crater.

"It's warm," she said.

"That's probably the sulfuric acid. Acid tends to make you warm," he said breezily.

"What? What?" She started to scramble out.

"I'm just kidding. I know nothing about the geology here, but I do remember reading that your government set off about two nuclear bombs every day in the 1960s here. So, you could be swimming in radioactivity. For that reason, I'm giving you a good two minutes before I join you. Just in case your skin starts peeling off your bones…or anything like that." He sat on the rock and took off his boots and socks. Even that felt good. "How's your skin? Has it started to loosen?"

She took a mouthful of water, bobbed up, and spat it at him. "I think I'm fine. It smells a little funky though. I doubt we can drink it."

"You just spat funky water at me?" he said, reaching for the zipper on his flight suit.

"To be fair, I didn't realize how funky it was until I had a mouthful of it," she said.

"I bet you say that to all the boys." He lowered himself into the water. It was warm, but not warm enough just to sit in as the temperatures dropped in the desert with the arrival of nightfall.

She splashed him in response. "Says the man who wants to get married on a beach."

"I absolutely, positively, do not wish to know about all the times you've had a mouthful of funky stuff. Some things are better left unsaid, especially before the marriage vows. After, however, I expect blow-by-blow details…demonstrations, maybe diagrams if you will."

"I'll bear that in mind."

"Come over here," he said.

She swam slowly toward him, and as she did, he realized that she had also taken off her bra. She stood up in the waist-high water.

"You're beautiful, you know," he said. He wanted to reach out for her, but he wasn't sure if he'd ever see her like this again, and he wanted to imprint it on his memory.

"Really?" She tried to cross her arms in front of her as if she were embarrassed, and then dropped them again.

"Why would you doubt it?" he asked, aching for her but wanting to prolong the moment.

"Because you keep saying things you can't possibly mean."

He frowned. "I absolutely mean everything I say."

He held his hand out for her and she took it, allowing him to draw her closer. "You know you're mine now," he said in the quiet of the evening.

"I think I do," she replied, her radiant face shimmering in the moonlight. Her words brought heat and certainty to his heart. He held her gaze for a few seconds before pulling her into his kiss.

Her mouth felt like home. Sure, warm, and welcoming. Her lips were soft on his, but her tongue challenging. He pressed against her, grabbing her ass, enabling her to wrap her legs around him, anchoring them at his back with her heels.

She pulled away from his mouth. "Do you think we'll die if we make love in a potentially radioactive pool of water?"

He stifled a laugh in her neck. "Die, or turn into ninja turtles."

She paused and slid a hand between their bodies to his dick. "I'll take the risk."

He took a shaky breath as her fingers stroked him. "You seem to have engaged your automatic throttle," she said.

All the blood was rushing away from his head. "I think *you* engaged it." He took another breath. "They were right about you. You have great stick control."

He lowered his head and found her nipple, erect in the cool evening air. He pulled it into his mouth, teasing it with his teeth and then the warmth of his tongue. All he could think was that he needed to be inside her, needed to own her for a time. Needed to hear her say his name as she came.

He trailed his fingers from her breasts, into the water, and between her legs. His dick could already feel her heat, and it would be oh so easy to just slide into her, with her legs wide open against him. His fingers found her clitoris, and every time he stroked it, her arse bobbed against his balls, making his brain fritz and his dick get harder.

Eleanor wanted him to ravage her. She felt wanton and free with him. She let go of his dick and stretched away from him, so she was floating on her back, her breasts buoyant. His fingers danced around her clitoris, then down to her ass, and back up to the center of her world.

Then he brought her hips a little lower in the water and slid into her with one stroke. Her back arched, and her nipples stiffened in the cool air. Air expelled from her lungs as she reveled in the total sensory feeling of having him inside her, with the cold air on her skin and the warmth of the water caressing her skin.

Her hands went to her breasts, taut and full in the water.

Her fingers plucked at her nipples as Dex stroked his dick in and out of her. His gaze found hers and he groaned. "You're like a fantasy, love. A fucking fantasy."

A frisson of pleasure shot through her at his words. She'd been one of the guys for way too long, and this man was truly forcing the woman inside out into the open. Sexy, natural, and open. Her body approved of the new feelings.

He thrust deeply inside her, grinding against her clitoris as he did. His hands held her ass in place, and for a second she wished he had three hands.

Holding his gaze, she put one hand between her legs and stroked her clit. His eyes dipped from her face, to her hand on her breast, to her fingers between her legs. His breath labored as he watched her, from his vantage point of being deep inside her.

Her fingers stroked herself, and then his dick as he pulled out, then herself again, and then her two fingers clasped around him as he plunged inside her. "Jesus," he whispered, increasing his tempo.

She ran her index finger over her clitoris, looking for her orgasm. It was right there. "Dex," she moaned as spasms overtook her. Her pussy grasped his dick in spasm, and her legs splayed in surrender. He thrust again into her, once, twice, and then groaned as he came, pulling her up and holding her close as his shudders wracked his body.

Eleanor was sated and triumphant. She wanted him to only think of her when he thought about sex. Only wanted him to see her pleasuring herself when he closed his eyes. Only wanted him.

CHAPTER TWENTY-TWO

They held each other in the pool—not saying much but feeling everything. At least Dex was. He couldn't let her go. Didn't want to. But her first shiver spurred him into action. He jumped out of the water and helped Eleanor out too. He grabbed his uniform T-shirt and used it as a towel on her, rubbing it across her skin, concerned that if either of them were wet when the temperature dropped, they'd both be in for an uncomfortable night.

She stood in front of him with a small smile on her face as he dried her off and giggled when his fingers slipped away from the T-shirt when he passed it between her legs. Her giggle turned into a moan as she stood dead still. He took a few seconds to absolutely ascertain the integrity of the drying process and then allowed her to do the same. Which she did in spades.

There was nothing hotter than being stroked through cotton. Illicit, and hot. He stopped her before he got too hard again. He wanted a whole day and night in a hotel room with her. Maybe a month. Maybe a lifetime.

They got dressed and pulled on their socks and boots again. There was little that would keep them warm tonight, except each other's body heat. He tried not to smile, reminding himself that they were stranded in the middle of a desert with little water.

Water. He bent to get the half bottle that was left. A small piece of rock jumped, blowing a tiny amount of dust in the air. He was moving before his brain had caught up with what he'd seen. He jumped at Eleanor, yanking her to the ground. "Sniper!" he yelled, even though she was underneath him.

Another sliver of rock exploded, close to his knee. "We're pinned." Adrenaline spiked through his blood. There was nothing scarier than being shot at by a sniper—he couldn't hear the gunshot, could just see the effect. Even if he couldn't hear the shot, he certainly could hear the vehicle heading toward them.

"We've got company," he said, moving his body fractionally so she could turn her head to see the truck barreling across the flat base of the valley. Dust spat up behind it, swirling like smoke.

"Can you reach the backpack?" she asked.

Nope. Not without being target practice. "Sure. Wait a moment." He slid off her and crawled, flat-out, like a crab, toward the bag. He hooked it in his elbow and made his way back. He knew his number was up if the sniper got closer than before; there was no reason why he couldn't pick them off now. But there was no shot. No chipped off rocks and no dust.

"Whoever it is, they're not trying to kill us," he said.

"Care to test that theory?" she asked, rooting around in the backpack.

"Not really."

"Okay, I will." Before he could say anything, she sat up, bag between her legs, and looked at the truck coming toward them.

"Fuck, do you have a death wish?" Now he just felt like a complete tool, lying down as if he were cowering from something she wasn't scared of. He sat up and joined her.

"He's pinning us down all right, but I think he's just keeping us in place so that these guys can get us." She pulled a Maglite from the bag they had taken.

"And that's your weapon of choice?"

She turned and smiled at him. "Only for the sniper."

Then he understood what she was doing. He pulled out his weapon and chambered a round. "It's going to be tricky."

"What have we got to lose?" She cocked an eyebrow.

"A beautiful wedding in Gretna Green?" he asked.

"What's Gretna Green?" She took her weapon from her pocket and charged it.

"It's where we will be eloping to. A town in Scotland where you can get married without any ceremony or license. It's like the Vegas of Europe."

"What makes you think I want to elope? What makes you think I don't want a huge dress, a huge cake, and eight attendants?"

"Well I'm certainly up for a huge cake." He shrugged. "Whatever gets you to the altar."

Her mouth dropped open. "Wait a minute, you don't think we're getting out of this alive, do you? You think we're going to die here in the desert at the hands of these… whoever is trying to kill us, and you'll never have to marry me. We'll be dead, won't we?"

"I'm hurt by your cynicism. And yes, maybe you're right, but it's got to say something that I'm at death's door and the only woman I want to marry is you." He tried not to smile.

"I'm the only woman here." She reached over and shoved him and he swayed away from her.

A rock exploded at their feet. "Shit. Now you're just trying to get me killed so you don't have to marry me."

"Sorry," she said. "Let's not…I can't do this banter now. I need to concentrate. We need to concentrate."

He nodded. The last thing he wanted to do was distract her.

The truck was so close he could virtually see the whites of their eyes. Or he would have been able to if it had been light. "I think it's dark enough to need your Maglite," he said.

"Yup. I just want them to get a little bit closer."

"Let's wait for them to get out of the truck. Then we will know how many there are, and how many we need to take out."

She turned to face him and reached out to cover his hand with hers. "I've dropped bombs, but this is a whole new reality for me."

He grabbed her hand and held it tight. "I know. I've got your back."

They stared into each other's eyes for a couple of seconds. Then the door of the truck slammed.

There were four people—men, actually. All had gotten out of the car with their hands on their sidearms. They were there to fight. They were there to kill them, like the team they had sent before.

Eleanor wanted to know who they were, why they were after them, why they had destroyed both aircraft. But she didn't think they were here to negotiate, or monologue as they always did in the movies.

She had to admit that if she was going to go down fighting, it made her feel a little better that she would be going down with Dexter. She wondered how much of what he was saying was true. She'd spent eight years without a companion, a partner. It was almost intoxicating to have Dex talk to her about marriage, even if he thought they were going to die. Even though she was literally the last woman on earth to him.

In a low voice he murmured, "Wait. Wait." He stretched out the second as long as he could. The men were about twenty feet away. He called to them. "We're unarmed. Are you here to rescue us?" Under his breath, and out of the corner of his mouth, he said, "I'm just checking their intentions. I thought it would make you feel better about killing them."

The men laughed. *Well that definitely makes it easier.* The

Maglite was in her left hand, and her weapon was on the ground beside her. Her hand was on it as if it was propping her up. The sniper could only be watching them through a night vision scope. By blasting the flashlight, she would be blinding him.

"Three, two, one," she said. She turned the Maglite on and aimed it where the sniper's shots were coming from. They both jumped up, and Dex took out the man closest to him on the right. Trying to keep the flashlight steady, she shot at the man in the middle, hoping that he was the head of the snake. He fell to his knees, then face-planted.

The man standing next to him reeled in shock and fumbled for his still-holstered weapon. Dex took out his knee with one round, making him fall to his side.

She leveled her gun at the last man standing. He hadn't reached for his gun, but he was eyeing them both, nervously swiveling his head between them.

Dex put up one hand. "Don't. We just want to talk."

He didn't reply but his gaze continued to flick between them.

"Who sent you? Who do you work for? Why do you want us?" Eleanor asked. "Tell us and we will let you go."

"And where will I go? How long do you think they'll let me live? They don't want any witnesses to this. None. No one." His hand went to his holster, but he only got his sidearm halfway out of the leather. Dex shot him.

Eleanor took a moment; she swallowed hard and looked at him. She could feel her chin trembling, and she bit her lip, because she wasn't going to cry.

"It's okay, Eleanor," he said. "That's a natural reaction."

She took a staggered breath and tried to swallow around the lump in her throat. It didn't work. Tears slid from her eyes. She used the flashlight hand to wipe them away, and she realized her mistake immediately. There was a sharp pinch below her collarbone, and an invisible hand spun her to the ground.

"Eleanor!" Dex shouted as he dove toward her.

"Did that bastard shoot me?"

"Don't talk, don't move." Dex pressed against the hole in her chest and it felt as if his whole hand was inside her. Her entire world went red with pain. She felt as if her life, and thoughts, and sight, and her soul were seeping into the ground beneath her.

Dex went into autopilot. He had nothing he could easily access that would stanch the flow of blood bubbling through her chest into her flight suit.

She had already passed out, but her heartbeat was still steady and strong. He grabbed the Maglite, shone it in the direction of the sniper, grabbed Eleanor by the scruff of her collar, and dragged her down the hill toward the truck. He stumbled and slipped on the small rocks, but he didn't care. It just made his journey faster.

He lay Eleanor on the ground with the truck between them and the sniper. He felt her pulse one more time before getting into the truck and looking for a first-aid kit. It was fast and shallow now. Her breathing was labored, but he didn't care—all that meant to him was that she was still breathing.

He found an old first-aid kit under the driver's seat. It was covered in dust and grime. Probably kicked a million times by the people sitting in the back of the truck. He opened it to find the contents were in as bad a shape as the box.

He grabbed the gauze and pushed it against the tiny wound. It looked like nothing. Like a pierced ear, but with the thick trickle of blood pulsing out of it. More gauze, and then a bandage around her to keep it in place.

She was still unconscious when he dragged her onto the backseat of the car. He was thankful she was, but scared as well. She had to live. She had to live.

He jumped into the driver's seat, beyond caring that the sniper could shoot him. Although the lack of shots, since Eleanor shone the light, suggested strongly that he had not properly recovered his night vision.

The rearview mirror had a compass set inside it, so he kept going southwest, which he hoped with all his heart was toward Nellis. Everything had been best guesses. Where they were, where they'd ejected, and where he was going now.

The moon was out—the one fortunate thing that happened to them in two days. It allowed him to see the rocks on the ground that he could drive around, and it allowed him to see the tracks the truck had made when they'd gone to kill them. His night vision was probably permanently shot after his ejection, but at least he could see that much.

He drove for an hour, first stopping every ten minutes to check on Eleanor, and then every twenty minutes. Her breathing was shallow and fast now. But he hoped that meant the bullet had not nicked her lung. She was still unconscious, and for the life of him he couldn't remember if that was a good or bad thing.

He imagined visiting her in the hospital. Bringing her flowers, flirting with the nurses only to see Eleanor rolling her eyes at him. He imagined taking her home to his home in the north of England. He imagined walking in the snow to the local pub and whistling to his dog. Because if he imagined their future, if it was cemented in his head, she couldn't die. Because their future was already there.

Darkness fell as a cloud drifted across the moon. It reduced his vision to what was in the headlights' beam. He had to slow down. Under normal conditions, his reflexes would have been good enough to take top speed through the desert, but with his lack of water, his damaged eye, and his injured ribs, he couldn't rely on his reflexes. Not when there was so much at stake.

Just as he fancied he could see the yellow haze in the sky of Las Vegas lights, the truck spluttered. It started to slow, and then the power cut out. The steering became heavy as it drifted to a stop. The fuel gauge was on empty. He thumped the steering wheel. Dammit. One of the shots must have caused a leak in the fuel tank.

Think about the future. Think about the future. It didn't work. He got out of the car and climbed in the back. He took a breath and felt for her pulse. She was still with him. He carried her out of the truck, feeling that the flat earth beneath her back would be better. He didn't want to think that it would be better for him to be able to perform CPR. Because that wasn't going to happen. She would wake up in an hour, groggy, with a smart comment.

He placed her carefully on the ground and looked up into the car for the backpack and water. And then realized that he'd been so worried about Eleanor, he hadn't picked up the backpack or the water when he'd shoved her into the truck.

He lay beside her and pulled her into his arms.

CHAPTER
TWENTY-THREE

It took all the energy she had to roll toward him. She held his hand and licked her lips with a dry tongue. Her chest felt as if her aircraft had landed on it. She knew she was getting weaker, and that meant she was dying. She was going to die because she had gotten emotional about killing people who'd been sent to kill her. If she had the energy, she would laugh. But if these were going to be her final hours alive, she wanted him to know.

"I'm so sorry."

He opened his eyes, and she saw his emotions flicker across his face. First shock that she was still alive, then concern, and then acceptance. The same acceptance that she'd already come to herself.

"Sorry for what?" he asked.

"For making you crash. For this." She felt as if a body were caving in on itself, incredibly fragile. Just how much blood had she lost anyway?

"You didn't make me crash, did you?" The frown on his face made her realize that he was in as bad a shape as she. He was trying to remember.

She didn't remember him being hurt. Except his ribs and his eye. But how long had they been without water? She couldn't remember. It could have been minutes, and it could have been days.

"I can't remember. But I remember thinking that I did." She was confused now. Why couldn't she remember what happened?

"You know, I might not remember exactly what brought us here, but I'm glad it did." He stroked her hand with his thumb.

She closed her eyes and swallowed. There was a strange relief in removing all pretense that they could survive this. She couldn't laugh but she pushed her cracked lips into a smile. "I guess we're stuck with each other, 'till death us do part.'"

"I wouldn't have it any other way." He closed his eyes and sighed. "For the past ten years, I've expected to die in a desert. I had no idea it'd be this one. In Vegas. I didn't even get to see a show," he said.

"Not even Britney Spears?" She coughed.

"It's such a waste of a trip." He wrapped her hand around his arm and held it close to his chest.

She nodded. "I get that," she whispered. There was a tickle in her throat, no, her chest maybe. She wanted to cough, but she couldn't. "Tell your mother you saved me in every way…except, of course, the literal way."

He tried to laugh, but it just came out as expelled air. "Ditto."

They lay there, not talking, just listening to each other's breath. She hoped she left first, thankful for the bullet wound in her chest. She didn't know how long they lay there; she just stared at the stars and the planes leaving beautiful vapor trails high in the sky.

She heard a noise, then voices. "Don't bother. They're already dead." A man's voice reached them. She couldn't move; she didn't want to move, not even her eyes when the man came within a few feet of them. She didn't want him to be the last thing she saw. She needn't have worried.

Dex sat up, his hand still gripping hers. "She's dead. I'm not."

"You're mistaken. You're both dead," the voice said.

Eleanor braced herself for the gunshot that would cruelly steal Dex from her in her final minutes. Her ears filled with the thrum of her heartbeat and what she thought was the last rush of blood through her body.

"What the fuck?" the man said instead.

Eleanor realized that the sound she had heard wasn't her body's last heartbeats, but the *whop-whop* of a helicopter. And the running engines of other vehicles.

There was a *thump*, and the man who'd been standing over them collapsed face-first next to Eleanor. She whimpered.

"It's okay," Dex said, but there was a level of doubt in his voice.

"Ironman! Ironman!" The voice came from up high. Sand

and debris flew over them. Dust saturated the air, and Eleanor closed her eyes, unable to breathe.

It was a sight for sore eyes. A civilian helicopter with the Animal hanging out the door and brandishing a semiautomatic. Plus there were three or four trucks, one with HERTZ written down the side filled with men and women in civvies. Dex may have been worried, but he doubted nothing if the Animal was involved.

Tinker and Ginger rushed out of one truck before it had stopped. Ginger took one look at him and shouted, "Water!"

In seconds Dex was sipping from an iced bottle of water, trying hard not to guzzle the whole thing. He held on to Eleanor's hand as two uniformed medics attended to her. She was unconscious again. He watched as they applied a rehydration drip and moved her to a stretcher.

"That was awesome!" the Animal said, still brandishing his weapon, but this time in the air.

They all probably wanted to tell him to "weapon down," but who had the heart?

Tinker began to explain. "We sat around for a full day, man. The exercises were canceled, and nobody said anything about where you were. So, we got a posse together, broke out of the lockdown, rented every vehicle from the stores outside the base we could find, including that one"—he pointed at a minivan still driving toward them—"and the Animal persuaded a female air ambulance pilot to come out here."

Then Ginger took over. "Of course, Tinker managed to persuade a guy in the control room to show us surveillance pictures from the Sentinel surveillance aircraft. We saw the tracks the truck made, and we were just following them when we found you."

Dex thanked God that he had decided to follow the truck's tracks backward from the hill where Eleanor was shot. The medics picked Eleanor up and headed toward a helicopter. Dex jumped up.

"There's no room," the Animal said. "You and I will have to hitch a ride back."

With his hand over his mouth, he watched the helicopter ascend with Eleanor inside. Tears stung his eyes.

Everyone was getting back into their trucks when the Animal pulled him aside with an uncharacteristically sober expression. "I don't know what happened out here, but remember you are a British pilot. Only the British are allowed to debrief you. There's something weird going on at Red Flag this year, so I suggest you have a rocky memory and insist on returning to the UK."

Dex nodded. Except there was no way he was going to leave Eleanor. "Can you get me to the hospital that they're taking her to?"

The Animal tipped his head to one side and looked at him for a couple seconds, probably understanding that his advice was going to go unheeded. "Sure. Of course, man." He clapped him on the shoulder and pointed at one of the trucks. "We'll take you."

As they started their journey to the hospital, Dex watched

the helicopter leave and head toward Las Vegas. Suddenly his ribs throbbed, and his eyes became too blurry to see through. Yeah, that's right: it was his ribs and his damaged retina. He closed his eyes and put his head in his hands.

Eleanor. Eleanor. Live. Live. Live. He said it over and over with every bump that jolted him.

CHAPTER TWENTY-FOUR

Eleanor awakened slowly, trying to figure out whether she was alive or dead. The pain would suggest she was either alive or in hell. She opened her eyes, blinking against the light and the white walls. There was a steady beep, which strongly suggested a heartbeat. Hell would have to wait for another day.

"Mrs. Daniels-Stone?" She turned her head to see a nurse in green scrubs holding a chart.

"No?" she croaked. *Daniels-Stone? Oh.* "Major Eleanor Daniels," she said.

The nurse frowned and looked at several other sheets of the chart. "I don't know what happened. Your name has been amended on all the sheets in handwriting."

"I have an idea," she whispered.

The nurse shook her head but adjusted Eleanor's bed and put a straw from a glass of water into her mouth. She drank thirstily until the nurse removed the straw. "You've just had a general anesthetic, so don't drink too much too quickly." The nurse looked over her shoulder. "There are people outside who want to talk to you. Are you feeling up to it?"

"How long have I been here?" she countered, trying to figure out if she could put them off until she spoke to Missy or—her heart clenched—Dex. Was he still here? Or had he already gone back to England?

"You were admitted four days ago. The operation took fourteen hours. You're lucky." She fluffed Eleanor's pillow. "I'm more than happy to tell them to go away."

She sighed, and winced. "I should probably get it over with."

The nurse opened the blinds a little to let in more light and turned to go.

"Wait. Has my father been to visit?" As soon as the words were out, she wished she could take them back. The look of pity the nurse gave her was too much to bear.

"No, Major." She took a buzzer from the bedside table and put it in her hand. "If you tire of talking to the gentlemen outside, just press it and I'll rescue you."

"Thank you," she said gratefully.

She heard the nurse give whoever was outside a stern warning about tiring her, and two uniformed men came in. A major from the Air Force Office of Special Investigations and a JAG—Judge Advocate General—who was for all intents and purposes a lawyer. She hoped it wasn't for her.

"Major Daniels, how are you feeling?" the major asked,

looking at his notes, which told Eleanor it was nothing more than a pleasantry.

"About how you would imagine," she replied in a low voice.

"Good, good. Now, we have some questions for you about the events that led you…well, here."

She looked at the JAG. "Why are you here?"

"I'm Lieutenant Colonel Janke. I've been assigned to observe the investigation."

She got the sense that the investigator wasn't happy about that. But he continued. "Flight Lieutenant Dexter Stone suggested that TechGen-One could have done something to your aircraft. Would you agree with his assessment?"

She was about to agree when Janke interrupted. "Do you know this man?" He flipped over his folder to show a photo of the man who had been on the golf cart in her hangar, and who'd pushed her in front of the limo, and who Dex had hog-tied in the desert.

"Yes. He tried to kill us in the desert. I saw him in my hangar. He was the one who was speaking to my father and Mr. Dan—" she started.

"I think we have what we need here." He turned to the investigator. "It's obvious he was working as a rogue agent. TGO's CEO said that he thought he might be slightly unhinged. He regretted hiring him and was considering firing him before this happened." He flipped his folder shut as if that was the end of it.

The major from Special Investigations looked pissed.

"When did Mr. Danvers talk to you about that?" he asked between tight lips.

The lieutenant colonel opened his mouth and then closed it again. He turned back to Eleanor. "How well do you know Major Missy Malden?"

Surprised, Eleanor hesitated. "Pretty well. She's a friend."

The investigator jumped in. "Could she have been working with the TGO agent"—he looked at his notebook—"Grove? Could she have allowed him to sabotage your aircraft? Looked the other way, even?" He spoke fast, as if he was prepared to be shut down at any moment.

Eleanor's head began thumping. "There's no way Missy's involved. I'd stake my life on that."

"But you can't prove that, can you?" Janke said with a level of inexplicable triumph.

"There's no way. Zero percent," she said. Her head was spinning so badly that she pushed the button the nurse had given her.

Her eyes closed, but she heard the investigator say, "I'm recommending we release Major Malden from custody. We have no evidence against her, nothing even circumstantial. And frankly, I don't appreciate you taking over my questioning. You're supposed to be observing."

If Eleanor had the energy, or will, she would have applauded the major for standing up to his superior, but she couldn't believe Missy was in custody.

"It makes no difference. We have our guy. He's a rogue agent. TGO isn't responsible for his actions, but they are good corporate citizens. They're taking full responsibility for the actions of this one man."

The investigator began to say something, but the door banged open, and they were ushered out. Eleanor wanted to ask questions, to speak to someone she trusted, but when she took a breath to ask the nurse, everything fell away into darkness.

The next time she woke up, it was dark outside. She wondered if she'd ever get her sleep pattern right again.

She tried to look through the blinds to see roughly what time it was. Although, it was hard to tell in Vegas.

"You're awake."

She started and realized Dex was sitting in a dark corner of her room, holding flowers.

Utter joy filled her heart. "You nearly gave me a heart attack," she said.

He took a breath and released it slowly. "You nearly gave me one. I thought I'd lost you." He put the flowers on the table and dragged the chair over to her bed. "Seriously. Stop crashing and being shot and stuff." He leaned in to kiss her.

She inhaled his scent and relaxed. He hadn't left.

"You stayed," she murmured.

He pulled away from her, a quizzical look on his face. "Of course I did. We all did. Until the investigators tied up their case, people have been taking turns guarding your door here. Even the guy whose nose you broke."

Tears sprang to her eyes. She had no words. "You stood guard?"

He shrugged. "They let me sit in here with you. I get the impression that not everyone in your squadron trusts me, but I'm prepared to win them over."

"You are?"

"I am." He brushed hair back from her forehead. "I'm not leaving you." He paused and swallowed. "I'm just not."

She squeezed his hand, reveling in the warmth and safety she felt with him. She was alive, not in hell, and Dex was still here.

And then she remembered the men who had been questioning her.

"Were you debriefed? An investigator and a JAG came to see me. They said that the guy with the long hair—Grove I think they said his name was—acted by himself. Could that be true?"

"They spoke to me, but I didn't have much to say. All I could tell them was what had happened to my aircraft. They seemed to be concerned with a woman called Misty, or Missy, or something. The JAG seemed convinced she was involved. But listen to me. My people have told me unofficially that we should not create waves here. They caught the guy who tried to kill you—and me, come to that—and if we want to continue flying, we need to bite the bullet and accept that they've caught the guy."

She nodded. Military life wasn't like civilian life. There were no inherent rights that allowed you to protest or to challenge an investigation. "Where's my father?"

Dex looked away. "I know he asked about you, but as far as I can tell, he was recalled to DC to work on a special project.

She nodded, unsurprised that he hadn't come to visit her. She realized that no matter what she did, he would always be concerned with himself first, his career second, and her a distant third. It surprised her that she didn't mind too much.

"The nurse tells me we got married while I was unconscious," she said with a smile.

"What's wrong with that? It's not as if I roofied you. Eh, don't worry. The hospital chaplain was strangely arsey about only one person being able to say the vows. We did, however, make a commitment to get engaged." His eyes went to her left hand.

She followed his gaze and found a white trash bag tie wrapped around her finger. She laughed, but a tear slipped down her cheek.

Dex rushed to her side and gently stroked the tear away. "I know it's probably not exactly your dream ring…"

She grabbed his hand. "It is. It's a perfect commitment to be engaged ring," she said.

"Because the janitor's closet had a whole array of these…rings. I could look for a different style if you like. I think he had blues ones too."

Yeah, she just wanted him to whisk her away right then. "Ask me properly, or I might see if the janitor wants to date me. I mean, since he has so many rings…"

Dex closed his eyes for a second, a small smile on his face. "Eleanor Daniels. Would you do me the honor of becoming my fiancée?"

She wanted to so badly, she just wanted to say yes. But

where was the harm in a little torture? "You don't think we should date first? Meet each other's parents?"

Dex shrugged. "I've dated a lot of girls. It's never worked out for me before, so why start now?"

"Oh, okay. You persuaded me, you smooth talker, you. Yes, I will get engaged to you. But, you know, much later."

EPILOGUE

Syria, eighteen months later

Eleanor was patrolling the no-fly zone in Syria, part of the coalition to push ISIS out of the country. It had been a long deployment, at least for her. But not anymore. She'd got back in the saddle six months after being shot. She'd had to show that her lung was healed and that she wasn't gun-shy, and that her reflexes were still better than Munster's, but without her father in the picture anymore, she was actually content not to take Killer's leadership position.

She and Dex had met every other month when they could—at the mercy of military rotator aircraft: more than one anticipated visit had ended with one of them being bumped from the aircraft because it was taking more cargo, or people more important than them. She shook her head. The number of times she'd had to give him a no-go call from the tarmac. But not anymore. He was due to Incirlik Air Force Base in Turkey any time now.

As if by thinking about him, a new aircraft entered the pattern. "Allied Sweeper One, entering the pattern," a familiar British voice said in her ear. Excitement flooded her body.

"About time you got here. I've been waiting nearly a year." She couldn't help herself from grinning ear to ear, and she was sure he could hear her smile over the airwaves.

"I'm worth waiting for," he replied in her ear.

"Bees has been waiting, pining, crying every night," one of her colleagues on the ground said.

"At least every night," she said with a smile. "Okay, let's keep channels clear." She heard a rally of clicks in her ear as they acknowledged her command.

They had been patrolling around the supply line, protecting aid workers and food convoys as they left Turkey and drove toward the Syrian villages that were being rebuilt. They were monitoring the airwaves on the ground and using signals and code to identify the people using the corridor of protection.

She just felt good, flying the pattern around the no-fly zone, protecting people instead of bombing them, knowing that Dex was close by. She swiveled her head, trying to see him even though she knew the no-fly zone was so big that it would be ridiculous to think she could. She'd known he was coming; she'd just anticipated meeting him on the ground first. So much for the sexy underwear she'd brought with her.

Ground control opened up a radio link. "We have a convoy of six trucks that we can't identify. Can somebody go check it out?"

"Roger that, Allied Sweeper One. Falling out of pattern. Send coordinates," Dex said.

Eleanor's blood ran cold. Of course he was the most capable pilot she had ever met, but it would be very typical of something to happen before he'd even got a chance to be in her arms again. "Patrol Three, falling in behind," she said into her radio.

"That's so sweet, you're scared for me." His voice was in her ear.

"Well if you go down, we go down together. It's our thing," she said.

"It certainly is."

She fell in behind his Typhoon. "You know your afterburner looks huge in that," she said.

"Don't say that. She'll hear you. She's quite sensitive to comments like that."

"It's a nice new ride," she said.

"Well, the other one had a few dings," he said.

She was about to reply something smart, but ground control interrupted. "Convoys picking up speed. We are trying to radio the vehicles in front of them to pull over or get out of the way, as a precaution. But this convoy could be ISIS, or ISIS sympathizers."

"Descending to three," Dex said.

"Descending to three," Eleanor repeated. "Roger that." This wasn't good. For four months, this passageway into the center of Syria had been kept clear. Wasn't it just fucking bad luck that the day Dex showed up, there was trouble?

"Executing flyby in three, two, one," Dex said.

She followed suit; as she was at the end of the convoy, she had a ping against aircraft. "Small-arms fire," she said, peeling off. "Ascending to five."

"I guess that takes the mystery out of it," he said. "Any damage?"

"All systems are good. Dials are steady," she replied. "I've had worse. But my maintenance chief is going to be pissed."

"Bees, what do you want to do?" Dex asked.

"That's a conversation for another time, but right now, how about I provide a distraction while you go finish it."

There was a pause, and Eleanor knew that Dex was thinking of another option.

"There's no time," she said. "I'm going in, so you better have my back."

She pulled back on the throttle and accelerated, banking right and entering the no-fly zone.

"On my way," Dex said.

She found the road and then the convoy. Farther up ahead, vehicles were pulling over to the side of the road. She slowed down as she passed those vehicles, giving the drivers and leaders of the convoy enough time to see her and to instruct whoever shot her before to try again.

She climbed just a little, enough to try limiting the small-weapons fire that she had taken before. The first round hit, pinging off a metal part of her aircraft. At three thousand feet above her, she heard Dex say, "Missile one release."

She banked sharply to the left and climbed for a few thousand feet. As she banked left, she swiveled her head right to see if Dex had hit the target. She saw the vapor trail of the missile as it centered on the first truck. All she could see from her vantage point was the lead truck jump in the air. The convoy stopped.

"Nice work. Are you just showing off for me a little?" she asked.

"Maybe a little. What did you say about my stick control?"

"I'm maintaining steady course at three," Eleanor said, rolling her eyes. Why couldn't they have just had a normal patrol, landed, and then had dinner at the chow hall? She shook her head. It would never be that easy.

"Allied Sweeper One, let us know when you've got a fix on the ground," she said.

She could see the vapor trail from Dex's brand-spanking-new Typhoon. "I'm doing a low pass. There seems to be men standing outside the trucks. What the...? I think I just saw a SAM tube poking out of the back of one of the trucks." A surface-to-air missile was nothing to play with.

Eleanor's blood ran cold. "I'm coming in," she said. Not hesitating for a second, she banked right and sharply descended. As she approached the convoy from the front, parallel to the road, she saw the missile deploy from the second track. "Missile loose, deploy flares!" she shouted.

"You shouting at me?" Dex said.

She was just about to shout at him again for questioning her when she saw his flares deploying at the same time he was annoying her. The missile exploded in the heat of the flares. The blast waved rattled her aircraft. Bastards. They better not try to kill her nearly-fiancé.

She deployed two of her own missiles, and as soon as they were loose, she pulled up in an almost vertical ascent. She felt a rattle as they exploded, but nothing more. She leveled out and came around to check the road again. All four vehicles were on fire. There were no people on their feet anymore.

"Targets are down," she said.

"Roger that," ground control said.

"Dex?" she asked. "How's it looking?"

"My new baby is definitely a little singed, but nothing worse."

Eleanor took a deep breath and shook her head. "Are all our dates going to be like this?"

"You mean chaos and destruction, paired nicely with the constant fear of death? I'm not going to lie, I'm looking forward to dinner and a movie."

She was about to reply when a new voice interrupted them. "Sniper One here to relieve," a voice on the frequency said.

"Allied Sweeper Six, here to relieve," another voice said.

They could go back.

"See you on the ground, Bees," Dex said.

Dex jumped out of his aircraft with about a tenth of the style and ease the Animal usually did. He'd been in his aircraft nearly all day and he was as stiff as a board. He'd flown from the RAF base in eastern England to the RAF base in Cyprus, where he'd refueled, and then he was supposed to land at Incirlik—the U.S. base—but he'd made an excuse to recce the patrol area.

He stretched gingerly, muffling a groan of pain.

"You old, old man," Eleanor's voice said.

He turned around. Wasn't she a sight for sore eyes? "I am, I admit it. But suddenly I feel like I'm eighteen again." He grinned and she ran toward him. She jumped on him, legs around his waist—bringing back instant memories of their time in the thankfully nonradioactive crater. "You missed me. That's so sweet," he said. "I didn't miss you at all, you know."

She laughed. "I could tell by the daily emails and the weekly calls. So negligent."

He kissed her and reveled in being close to her, feeling her lips, smelling her scent. He was home. Even if they were in the middle of Turkey. He'd never been so happy to give up a life of military flying. He would have given up anything to be able to see her every day. And the truth was, he'd handed in his papers and hadn't regretted it, or felt sad, or anything. His life wasn't the military anymore—it was Eleanor Daniels-Stone.

He had two months of rotation here in Turkey, and then he turned in the keys to his Typhoon. And then he'd go wherever she was going.

"I was saving this, but I have my new assignment. It's at RAF Mildenhall." She grinned at him and he took a breath. Mildenhall was in England. He could have stayed in the military. He gave himself a beat to process the information.

Nope. Nothing. He wasn't resentful, upset, or angry. He was the happiest fucker in the whole of England.

"You're going to love England, sweetheart. I'm going to love seeing it through your eyes." His smile dissolved. "I'm going to love seeing everything through your eyes." He nodded. "It's perfect. Everything's perfect. *You're* perfect."

Eleanor tipped her head to the side. "I think we both know that I'm not perfect—but you'll definitely get laid for saying so."

"And now my life is complete." He kissed her again.

She pulled away from him. "I can make it just a tiny bit more complete." She bit her lip and pointed over his shoulder.

He turned around. The base chaplain was pacing up and down a short trajectory, obviously waiting for them to stop kissing. He turned back to her, wondering what she meant.

"Well…in order for us to get married quarters…"

He looked back at the awkward-looking chaplain. "You bought me a chaplain? That's so sweet. I mean, it was on my Christmas list but…"

She gave him a "shut your mouth" look.

She put her fingers on his lips and he shut the hell up. "Are you willing to make an honest woman of me?" She stood back and put both fists on her waist.

"You bet your arse I am, sweetheart. Catch." He threw a small box at her and she plucked it out of the air without breaking eye contact. Man, she was the coolest fiancée any man could ever have.

She opened the box, and her hand flew to her throat as she found a totally legit, real non-janitor-closet engagement ring. She stepped to him and kissed him. "Let's do this."

He grinned and held out his arm to her. She put hers in his, and they went to meet their chaplain. He was going to be a husband today. He punched the air in total victory.

She laughed at him. Life was good.

PLEASE SEE THE NEXT PAGE FOR
A PREVIEW OF

Wingman

COMING IN SUMMER 2017

CHAPTER ONE

Major Missy "Warbird" Malden shifted uncomfortably and looked around her holding cell. It was pretty clean, all things considered. Not that she'd had much experience with cells, other than those she'd seen on TV. At least this one didn't have a toilet in the corner.

But clean or not, this was not where she'd thought she would be two days into the Red Flag exercise. She should be up in the skies, directing missions and worrying about how to tell her front-seat pilot, Lieutenant Colonel Francis Conrad, that she was requesting a transfer to another squadron. For…reasons. Her heart clenched in her chest as she realized how badly she'd screwed everything up.

At least she didn't have to worry about that anymore. She was pretty sure that being arrested under suspicion of espionage was going to put the chocks on her career. Especially since she couldn't defend herself from the accusation. Or suspicion, or whatever it was that had landed her there.

Maybe Delta would be hiring in fifteen to twenty years for good behavior. Except they would probably also have a problem with someone who had allegedly caused a couple of aircraft to crash.

She tensed. She'd been so worried about herself that she'd forgotten about Eleanor. And the British pilot, both of whom had crashed in the desert. For some reason the three-star general on base—and Eleanor's father—had automatically assumed it was sabotage and that Missy was the prime suspect.

Please be alive. Please be alive. They hadn't been found yet, which she hoped was a good sign. Finding wreckage was relatively easy, but she had no idea why they hadn't been able to ascertain where the pilots were. She clenched her fists. There was something off about all this.

She jumped up instinctively as the door clanged open. A man in dress blues entered, a thick file beneath one arm. "As you were." He nodded back to her chair.

She sat, as was ingrained habit. His emblem told her he was a lieutenant colonel, the name on his badge said "Janke." He outranked her.

"I've been assigned as your JAG in this matter," he said, sitting and then flipping open the folder with a pen.

Shit just got real. She was legitimately a suspect. Somehow she'd expected someone to open the door and let her go. Apologize for the mistake. She'd half thought it would be Conrad, the one person on earth who knew what had happened that night, aside from Missy. And she, herself, wasn't entirely sure what had happened that night, nor what it meant.

"What exactly is it that I'm being accused of? If someone would just tell me, I could clear this up pretty quickly, I'm sure." She held her hands out in an appeal. This whole thing was out of control. She just wanted to get back to her aircraft, get airborne, and help search for Eleanor and the British pilot.

"Sir," he said.

What? "I'm sorry—"

"You forgot to say 'sir.'" He leaned back in his chair. "Do you make it a habit of disrespecting your superior officers?"

She frowned. She hadn't come across an officer with that kind of attitude in ten years. She forced her face into a blank expression. "No, sir. I apologize."

He stared at her, his dark eyes cold, empty almost.

The enormity of her situation hit her hard. Conrad wasn't coming for her, and as much as she had joked to herself about a fifteen-to-twenty stretch in jail, she'd been convinced this whole ordeal would be over within hours. A feeling of dread seeped through her, rendering her hands and feet icy-cold. She flexed her fingers.

"All you have to tell us is where you were last night." He pulled a tight smile and reopened the file on the table between them. "And tell us everything you know about TechGen-One and General Daniels."

She fought not to do a double take. *What?* Why was he asking about TechGen-One and Eleanor's father? Suddenly, a whole battery of thoughts whirled in her head. The military contractors who had been in their hangar on the first day of Red Flag doing a "security check." The conversation

Eleanor said she would have with her father. But that…that was it. She had nothing. "I don't know anything about TGO except what everyone knows, sir. They saved Red Flag from being canceled. As for General Daniels…I've…" She paused. Why was her lawyer interrogating her?

"Colonel Janke. Why don't you tell me what the charges against me are? I mean, you did say you were my assigned JAG, didn't you?" She paused. "Sir." This was total bullshit.

He rose slowly and gave her a smile. A pitying, condescending smile. But even that couldn't disguise the jumping vein in his neck. "This is the moment, Major." He nodded. "This is the moment you will look back on for the rest of your life—no matter how long or short that may be—and you'll wonder if your answering my two simple questions would have saved you."

She didn't like that he paused after the word *short*. She didn't like anything about this. "Are you threatening me, sir?"

He moved fast, banging his fists on the table. She jerked back from him and then cursed herself for showing her fear.

"I never have to threaten, Major." There was a pause—a silence that hung in the air.

Missy forced herself to hold his gaze. "I want a different JAG."

A line wrinkled his forehead, and she was sure she saw a flash of panic in his eyes. He straightened. "Just those two questions, and I'll make sure you'll be back in barracks by sunset."

Her gut told her not to trust him. If Conrad had taught

her one thing, it was to listen to her gut. "I want a different JAG," she repeated.

He took a step toward her, and she scraped her chair loudly away from the table and stood.

Colonel Janke looked her up and down, not lasciviously, but maybe wondering how much she'd fight back.

She took a step toward him, forcing him to take one backward. She wanted him to know she would fight back.

Whatever the hell this was, she wasn't going down without a fight.

ABOUT THE AUTHOR

Emmy Curtis is an editor and a romance writer. An ex-pat Brit, she quells her homesickness with Cadbury Flakes and Fray Bentos pies. She's lived in London, Paris, and New York, and has settled for the time being in North Carolina. When not writing, Emmy loves to travel with her military husband and take long walks with their Lab. All things considered, her life is chock-full of hoot, just a little bit of nanny. And if you get that reference...well, she already considers you kin.

Learn more at:
  EmmyCurtis.com
  Facebook.com/EmmyCurtisAuthor
  Twitter @EmmyCurtis19

9 781478 947905